Archibald Clavering Gunter

Small boys in big boots : a story for children of all ages

Archibald Clavering Gunter

Small boys in big boots : a story for children of all ages

ISBN/EAN: 9783337215682

Printed in Europe, USA, Canada, Australia, Japan

Cover: Foto ©Andreas Hilbeck / pixelio.de

More available books at **www.hansebooks.com**

SMALL BOYS IN BIG BOOTS

A STORY
FOR CHILDREN OF ALL AGES

BY

ARCHIBALD CLAVERING GUNTER

AUTHOR OF "MR. BARNES OF NEW YORK," "MR. POTTER OF TEXAS,"
"THAT FRENCHMAN," ETC.

NEW YORK
THE HOME PUBLISHING CO.
1890

CONTENTS.

LIST OF ILLUSTRATIONS.

FROM ORIGINAL DRAWINGS BY DAN. BEARD, C. HILLS WARREN, A. D. BLASHFIELD, AND JOHN LYTH.

SMALL BOYS IN BIG BOOTS.

CHAPTER I

"MA! may I go on the stage?"

At this astounding question from a girl of thirteen her widowed mother, pretty Mrs. Effie Bushnell, after a gasp of astonishment, cries: "Go on the stage, Myra? You have never even been inside a theatre."

"Yes, I have—the Peekskill Opera House!" cries Myra, enthusiastically.

"The Peekskill Opera House! What do you mean?" stammers Mrs. Bushnell.

"I mean this, mother dear—Teddy Rawson and the boys have made Rawson's old barn into a theatre—the Peekskill Opera House. They've been playing there two weeks, and the next is to be a *grand* production. Arthur is to be a super, and Laura Haughton is to be an actress, and I want to be one too—and—and—they've got Footlights for—for—manager and star."

Here Myra stops for want of breath, and her mother asks, curiously : " Who is Footlights ? "

" You—don't—know—who—Footlights—is ? " The girl's voice comes slowly and her brown eyes open wide with astonishment. " Footlights is as celebrated—as Barnum and Buffalo Bill—and acts with them."

" Nevertheless, I have never heard of the celebrated Footlights," remarks Mrs. Bushnell, with a slight smile.

" Then I'll tell you all about him," babbles Myra, enthusiastically. " Footlights's real name is Jemmy Higgins. You used to know his mother ; she used to do washing for you four years ago. Jemmy's been down to New York, and has been an actor with Booth and Barnum and Barrett. He's come here for the summer to visit his father, the brakeman, and has kindly consented to manage the theatre for Teddy Rawson and the boys. I had supposed you must have known all about him and seen him on the stage, he's *so* celebrated. Ma, doesn't Captain Heaton *ever* take you to the theatre, in New York ? "

At this sudden mention of Captain Heaton's name Mrs. Bushnell reddens with blushes, but does not answer.

So Myra goes on, recklessly and sarcastically : " Well, I wouldn't give a cent for a fellah who didn't take his best girl to theatres and ice-cream restaurants. I'd give him the *grand bounce !* I'd—oh ! ma !—what's the—mat- mat—ter ? I—don't look at me so ! Oh ! what have I done ? Oh, ma ! Don't, please ! "

For, at these extraordinary sentiments, her mother has turned very pale and an expression has come into her face that makes Myra tremble. " Where did you get those awful ideas ? " she cries. Then striding up to the shivering culprit, Effie Bushnell, forcing herself to calmness, says : " And what do you mean by your remarks about ' best girl ' and ' fellah ' and ' giving him the grand bounce ' ? "

"Nothing, ma! Nothing—I—only got them from the new story that I'm reading."

"What story?"

"'The Gayest Boy in New York!' Teddy Rawson lent it to me. I've just finished 'The Human Vampire' and 'Smart Aleck.' They're lovely!"

"Are they?" remarks her mother, dryly. Then she says, suddenly, as if a flood of light had just broken in upon her: "Myra! I have often wondered what caused the curious remarks you have made for the last month and gave you your extraordinary ideas of life. Now I understand it. You've been reading books that are poison to young minds ; that make you precocious without wisdom, and vulgar without wit. You will take those books back to Teddy Rawson, who is a very bad boy and got your brother Arthur punished by taking him off fishing and making him late for school."

"But, ma, Teddy says that if Arthur had had any sand——"

"Hush! There's another slang expression from those horrid books. I found one of them yesterday, though I had no idea you read such things. This is it, I believe." And, opening a drawer in her escritoire, Mrs. Bushnell produces a pamphlet with a ferocious picture on its cover, and entitled, "The Secret League of Seven ; or, Six Murders and One Hanging," and says, with a very serious voice, "Have you read this?"

"Yes!" gasps Myra, for her mother's manner frightens her.

"Very well! If I discover you reading any story you do not bring first to me for my approval, I shall punish you—do you understand me?"

"Yes, mamma." The child's lips are pouting, for she dearly loves the uncanny sensations and exciting absurdities of these atrocious stories that have made fools of so many boys and girls

in America: literary trash, that, planted in youthful minds, is poi-
sonous as the upas-tree of Java; bringing not only death to any
true moral tone, but destruction to childish common-sense; making
this every-day world of ours a lurid and unnatural dream, where
boys of tender age turn bandits and freebooters, and girls have
amourettes and romantic attachments before they are out of short
clothes. Myra already viewed the world through a dime-novel
eye-glass; a distorted lens that has made some boys, when they
should have been saying, "Now I lay me down to sleep," by their
bedsides, sneak out into the night to become criminals; and has
driven little girls, who should have been shedding the tears of
childhood on their mothers' breasts, to commit even suicide.

"Remember what I have told you!" repeats Mrs. Bushnell, as
Myra, concealing a sob in the lower part of her throat, is leaving
the room.

At the threshold the girl turns and says: "But you haven't said
I could play in Footlights's theatre, mother?"

"No!" answers Effie, shortly; "you can't play in Footlights's
theatre. Your school will begin in a week! Besides, Myra," here
the mother comes to her and takes her in her arms, "I want my
little girl to be a child as long as she can; and such amusements
tend to make her precocious——"

"Then I can't be an actress?"

"Certainly not! But, Myra, if you are a good girl I shall tell
Susan to give you——"

"What?"

"Ice-cream for dinner."

"Don't want any!"

"No?"

"Not much! I saw the bakery man bring it into the house
half an hour ago—and I've eaten all I want already. Mother,

can I play on the stage—*just once?*" and Myra is all entreaty again.

"I have already answered you, NO!" returns Mrs. Bushnell, sharply, for she is annoyed at her daughter's inroad on the family dinner. "Myra, don't cry so!"

To this last she gets no answer, for the little girl has burst from her in a paroxysm of pouts and tears. Her mother gazes after her, slightly sighs, and mutters to herself: "I must give more thought to my children—Heaven would not forgive me if I forgot them in my love for Cyril. Could Myra have meant to insinuate—" Here the beautiful widow blushes, and then remarks to herself: "I presume even Myra knows, by this time. It's just as well—perhaps better, that she does."

As for the child, recovered from her tears, among the flowers and trees of her mother's beautiful country-place, River View, at Peekskill-on-the-Hudson—for she had betaken herself and her fancied wrongs to the solitude of the garden—her face grows savage and she mutters: "Mother's down on me because I teased her about being Captain Heaton's best girl—she's awful sweet on him. Teddy Rawson says he's going to be my step-father. Step-fathers are always cruel! Oh, how I hate him! He shan't marry my ma! O-o-oh!" and Myra goes into another spasm of childish despair.

Leaning against an elm-tree, notwithstanding the tears that stream down her face, the little girl makes a pretty picture as the September sunlight falls upon her. She has bright brown eyes and chestnut hair, and her face denotes that some day she will exchange the beauty of childhood for the beauty of womanhood, and then she will have a strong character--either good or bad. This will greatly depend upon her training during the next few years. She is very tastefully costumed in a light summer muslin frock with a big bow of blue ribbon. Under its short skirt, her graceful feet and ankles, in light stockings and slippers, can be seen, for she is still dressed as a child.

After a few moments she grows calmer, then mutters : " I'll—I'll consult Teddy, he'll give me a pointer on Captain Heaton."

With this, she runs off through the garden to a little gate leading into the grounds of an adjoining villa, hurriedly drying her eyes, though there is a resolute gleam in them that bodes ill to her mother's second romance.

Mrs. Effie Bushnell's marriage engagement had come about in this way ; for Myra, with the precocity of childhood, had guessed correctly.

The pretty village of Peekskill, overlooking from its green heights the beautiful Hudson River, is the location of the New York State Camp of Instruction. Each summer, regiment after regiment of its National Guard march upon its parade-ground in rotation, and for a week practise in this school of the soldier.

Mrs. Effie Bushnell was the widow of a retired New York merchant who had purchased a pretty country-place near the village, and taken his young wife there some dozen years before the day of Myra's histrionic aspirations.

When Anson Bushnell had married Effie Livingston, he had been a man of fifty, and she a girl of eighteen. On his death, two years before the scene that has just taken place, he had left her with a very comfortable provision for his children, safely invested in gilt-edge securities.

These children were Myra, now thirteen ; Hettie, a tot of seven ; and Arthur, a studious boy of twelve. Consequently, though the mother of a family, Effie Bushnell was only thirty-two, and too young and beautiful to hope to be permitted to live entirely for her children ; though it can be truthfully said she had devoted herself to them, until one bright summer's day her carriage had drawn up

"OH, TEDDY! TEDDY! MA WON'T LET ME BE AN ACTRESS!"

beside the drill-ground, and she had watched the dress-parade of the gallant Twenty-second. The band inspired her, the white coats of the regiment dazzled her, and Captain Heaton, as he marched at the head of his company, seemed the most commanding and soldierly warrior of them all.

Soon after this an introduction came about, and the pretty widow's victoria was seen daily at dress-parade, and though the regiment, after its week's service, marched home, Captain Cyril Heaton came back, and before the end of the summer it was rumored about Peekskill that Mrs. Effie Bushnell was soon to become his wife.

After passing the little gate, Myra walks through an avenue of maple and elm which, taking a turn or two, leads her to an old barn. Just before she arrives at this, she is met by a red-faced, jolly-looking boy, clad in comfortable knickerbockers. To him she hurriedly runs, and in accents of despair cries : " Oh, Teddy ! Teddy ! ma won't let me be an actress !"

"Won't she ? " says the young gentleman addressed, rather slowly and with some difficulty, for he is eating a banana, and his mouth is very full. " Why don't you do it, anyway ? Defy her ! That's what Matilda Hotshot did in the 'Boys of New York.' Tell her she's a blarsted tyrant, and—*defy her !* " This last is said in a melodramatic manner, for, to give proper effect to his speech, Teddy has bolted the remainder of his banana.

"I—I daren't," mutters Myra, who has grown pale at the suggestion. " She—she threatens to punish me if I read any more of those lovely books you lent me."

" Afraid of mammie, eh ? " sneers Teddy. " Myra, you've got no grit—who wouldn't take a licking to play in *that* drama ? " And he points proudly to a placard on the entrance to the barn, in front of which they now stand.

It is in red paint and has been daubed upon an old piece of white cotton cloth : apparently a fragment of a disused sheet.

At this Myra now gazes, reading it with a sad and longing ecstasy, for it is :

CHAPTER II.

"I CAN DO IT!"

AFTER gazing at this flaming announcement till tears of longing come into her eyes, Myra says, huskily : "Teddy, you tell Footlights I shall not go on the stage—I—I can't." With this, the child breaks down and gives a sob.

"Don't be a muff!" cries Teddy. "Go in and tell him yourself. He's at work on the scenery."

"On the scenery! How lovely! Painting it?"

"No! *Chopping* it!"

At this astounding announcement Myra's eyes open with astonishment, as she asks, "How?"

"How? In the regular way, of course, like in all big theatres. In small, *cheap* theatres they have only imitation scenery—painted stuff! Now Footlights is going to have the *real* thing. We want trees to surround the drill-ground of the State Camp. In low-down places of amusement they would paint 'em on canvas. We went out, cut all the trees we needed, and now Footlights is chopping them to fit, and nailing them upon the stage. We've stole a real sentry-box and carted it down in Sam Corbin's wagon, and it's to be the guard-house and general-headquarters. Footlights is a realist of the most advanced type. He's going to have real guns, real powder, real water, and *real blood!*"

"Real blood! How do they want real blood for a militia play?"

Unheeding Myra's unconscious sarcasm upon our State troops,

Teddy goes on : "*Real* blood, I tell you! Our property-man, Tim
Jones, is going to make his nose bleed for the real blood when
Captain Wiggins kills Captain Jinks in a hand-to-hand sabre duel.
Real blood!"

"Oh, how lovely!" cries Myra. Then she mutters, "And I

can't act in it!" Next, after a little choked-down sob, she asks,
very, very anxiously : "Will Footlights raise the price of admission?" for the child longs more and more for the distracting
delights of the drama the farther she thinks herself from them.

"Come in and ask him. And you'd better tell him you've

given up the stage, if you're going to let your mother bully you out of it. I've read of girls running away from home for much less !" remarks Teddy.

Following him into what was once Rawson's barn and is now " The Peekskill Opera House," Myra finds herself in the presence of the august Footlights.

This shining dramatic star is, perhaps, a year older than Teddy, though hardship has taken from his face the freshness of youth, and the struggle for bread has given to his fifteen-year-old countenance an expression of precocious tact and perhaps cunning. For Jemmy Higgins had been born of poor but honest parents, and had suffered accordingly.

His father for many years had been a station-hand at the New York Central Depot at Peekskill, and Jemmy had lived with his parents there for the first twelve years of his life. Then his mother had died, and the boy, left almost to his own resources, had sought a livelihood in the great city of New York. There he had, curiously enough, become an *attaché* of the theatrical profession, being at one time tent-boy at Barnum's circus, at another lemonade-vender in Buffalo Bill's Wild West at Staten Island, and afterward programme-boy at a Bowery theatre. This place of amusement being closed for the summer vacation, and still remaining unopened, early in September, Jemmy had come to spend the time with his father, filled with a precocious knowledge of the world in general and theatrical matters in particular that had made him the delight and envy of the boys of the place. Jemmy's anecdotes of the stage, in which he modestly figured beside Booth, Barrett, Salvini, Buffalo Bill, and Barnum, as a different but certainly not *lesser* star, had gained for him an extraordinary reverence from the boys with whom he condescended to associate, and they had given him the significant epithet of " Footlights," not as a term of derision but as an attribute of intense esteem. For most boys have in their hearts an inbred love of the drama and a mysterious awe, mingled with an all-absorbing curiosity, for those realms of indescribable beauty and magnificence—"behind the scenes."

His general knowledge of matters theatrical had been made the most of by the precocious Footlights, for he had, with the assistance of Teddy, converted an unused barn attached to the Rawson country-house into a juvenile theatre, upon the stage of which the youthful Footlights strutted as star, and the profits of which changed the pocket-money of his youthful admirers into the pocket-money of Footlights, the youthful manager.

This theatrical venture had been very successful for several weeks, the profits of Saturday performances being sometimes as high as two or three dollars. These receipts, and what he could get from his father, had kept the youthful tragedian in—to him—comfortable circumstances, for, practising stern economy, Footlights's stage was his bed, and his drop-curtain his blanket, and he compelled the members of his company to bring their suppers or lunches with them when they came to rehearsal, kindly condescending to share their meals with them.

Tempted by fortune, the youthful manager is now about to see if he cannot appeal to older and longer pockets than those of his young admirers, and is about to risk his financial fate on the issue of a grand production. He is placing on his stage an original drama, "The Hero of the State Camp!" This piece is the joint concoction of himself and the ambitious Teddy; Teddy furnishing a plot stolen and adapted from various ferocious dime-novels, and replete with the humor of this peculiar literature, in which small boys whip grown men and lads play audacious tricks upon their parents. These materials have been made use of by Footlights, who has injected a military hero and masher into the play—*Captain*

Hotspur Wiggins—to carry the hearts of all damsels by storm, especially that of a beautiful Peekskill maiden, whom he marries after defending her from the plots and intrigues of a military villain, one *Captain Redfern Jinks*, a *rôle* for which he has cast his collaborator, Teddy Rawson.

Footlights, in conjunction with several members of his company, boys large and small, is engaged in his stage preparations as Myra approaches. The place is a scene of dramatic disorder and resembles, as the girl gazes at it, a mixture of theatre and of barn ; the place set aside for the audience having benches made of rough boards that have been placed upon provision-boxes of assorted sizes. Two of the stalls originally used for horses have been converted to theatrical uses by cheap draperies, apparently contributed from the houses of some of the company, and are marked " Box A " and " Box B." The stage itself is constructed of the partitions of several other stalls that have been torn down and placed upon two large horse water-troughs to elevate it some eighteen inches above the floor of the auditorium.

The back wall of the stage has been painted a cerulean blue to represent the sky ; but this effect is slightly marred by the huge beams of rough timber that spread their supporting arms through the atmospheric effect. In front of this, upon the stage, a number of natural trees, cut down for the purpose, have been placed in a semicircle, giving to the stage a rustic appearance ; while the military effect is produced by the stolen sentry-box, upon which has been nailed a Fourth of July American flag.

Two or three girls are seated in the auditorium, gazing in rapt attention at the preparations being made. One of them, catching sight of Myra, runs to her and unintentionally stabs her cruelly, for she whispers : " Ain't it glorious ? You should have seen the rehearsal to-day. Why weren't you here ? Oh ! it was gorgeous—those love-scenes between Footlights and me. Myra, have you ever seen him make stage-love? It's so terribly intense; he hisses all he says, and he scowls at you awful. It's simply perfect. You should have heard him hiss at me: 'Be mine, or I'll make you rue the day you loved another military man!' And then, my costume. I've borrowed mother's pearl-silk dress for mine. It's got a train! Oh, Myra, fancy—a train!" And then the girl, who is perhaps a year older than Myra, adds the last drop of misery to the child's cup, for she asks, "What are *you* going to wear?"

"I ain't going to wear anything!" g r o w l s Myra, savagely; "I ain't going to act. Ma says——"

"She'll whack her if she plays," interjects Teddy, "and the little girl hasn't got the grit to take the chances!"

"How can you tell such fibs, Teddy Rawson?" answers Myra. "Ma never said she'd whack me in——"

"DON'T YOU KNOW STAGE LANGUAGE?" SNEERS FOOTLIGHTS.

But here they are interrupted from the stage. Footlights has rushed to the centre of it, and is calling wildly, "Props! Props!"

"Props for what?" yells Teddy. "Great Scott! Is the roof coming down?" And in a moment the whole company are around their youthful manager in dismay.

"Don't you know stage language?" sneers Footlights. "By Props, I mean the property-man, Tim Jones."

At this a white-headed, gawky boy of about sixteen, all legs and arms, for he is nearly six feet high, says: "What do you want, Mr. Manager?"

Then the manager haughtily says: "I want two more trees cut down to mask in the hay-rack, and two lengths of clothes-line to hang the sky upon—" and points to several strips of muslin painted blue.

"Where'll I get the clothes-line?" asks Tim Jones.

"That's your business to find out. Ain't you the property-man?" remarks Footlights, as if that settled the question.

"I'll tell you where," suggests Teddy. "You hook one from Sam Thomas's mother—she's got lots of clothes-lines. And, Sam Thomas! you go and help him."

"All right," answers Jones. "Mrs. Thomas won't drop to our racket if she sees me playing in her yard with her son Sammy. Come along, Sammy!" And he departs for his raid on Sammy's mother's goods, attended by little Sammy himself, a precocious boy of about ten.

Upon all this Myra gazes with melancholy interest. This excitement is not for her. She is no longer one of the company.

This business being settled, and the various members of his force being engaged about the stage, Footlights turns suddenly to Teddy and says, sharply: "Throw that 'ere cigarette away!"

"What for?" asks the boy, who has been engaged in preparing for himself one of those small doses of physical poison.

"Because the rules of *my* company forbid smoking on the stage!"

answers the juvenile manager, sternly. "Toss that cigarette away, and *read 'em!*" and he points to a placard pasted up at the back of the stage.

The tone of his voice is so commanding that Teddy obeys him in a sheepish way as he whispers to Myra, who is astonished at his meekness: "Discipline must be kept up for the benefit of the rest of the company." Then he and the girl read as follows:

STAGE RULES OF THE PEEKSKILL OPERA HOUSE

1st All members of the company must be on time at rehearsals or they will be fined five Cents. No excuse of being Kept at home by parents or teachers will be allowed

2nd All members of the company attending rehearsals at noon time will bring their lunches with them and. Deposit them with Manager

3rd No Swearing, fighting, Cigarette, Cigar Smoking or ungentlemanly or unladylike actions will be allowed.

4th No back Talk will be taken upon the Stage!

5th All fines payable in cash to the Manager

N.B. These rules are made for the discipline of the Company, the Manager being on his own prem-ises will do as he Pleases

James Higgins Sole Proprietor & Manager

While they have been reading, Footlights has been consulting a dirty memorandum-book which he has produced from a well-worn, seedy, and threadbare jacket, and his voice now comes to the girl in awful tones: " Myra Bushnell, juvenile actress, is fined ten cents for not being at rehearsal to-day ! "

" Ten cents," gasps Myra; " I—I came to tell you that mother won't let me go on the stage."

" Not go on the stage ?" ejaculates Footlights, in tragic tones. " Not go on the stage ? Shall I, then, have to cut out the part ? This is cruel ! "

" And if you fine me," continues Myra, huskily, " perhaps I— I won't have money enough to buy an admission to your perform-ance, and I—I should so love to see you play *Captain Hotspur Wiggins.*"

At this delicate compliment the face of the young Thespian assumes a smile, and he remarks, generously : " Never mind, little girl, I'll let you off the fines."

" Will you, though ? That's lovely !" cries Myra. "Oh, won't you look beautiful in uniform ! "

" In uniform !" gasps Footlights. " Great Barnum ! I—I had forgotten that ! A costume ! Two military bang-up costumes— one for you, Teddy, and one for me. They'll cost a dollar apiece to hire. By the living Jumbo, this busts the show !" And, with a hollow groan from the bottom of his heart, the tragedian assumes a tragic attitude.

This groan is echoed by Teddy, and reëchoed by some of the other youthful actors who have been listening. They now crowd about him with various suggestions. The company's funds are counted hastily, and found lacking.

" If Dazian would only do it on tick," mutters Footlights. Then he shakes his head mournfully and mutters: " No, Dazian might trust Booth or Daly for two dollars, but I'm hardly up to their standard." Then he gasps : " Two bang-up dress militia uniforms— that's what'll bust ' The Hero of the State Camp.' "

" Two uniforms !" repeats Myra, who has looked upon the tragedian's despair in sympathy and sorrow. Then a sudden, excited flash comes into the little girl's eyes, and she cries, " I CAN DO IT !"

" Do it? You?" This is a yell from all.

" Yes. I can get them ! Two bang-up Twenty-second Regiment's officers' uniforms !"

" You can !" screams Footlights. Then he mutters, savagely : " Don't play with a desperate man. You don't mean it ?"

" I do mean it -every word of it !"

" Very well; you do it, and I'll make you head wardrobe-woman to the Peekskill Opera House, with free admissions for the season !" answers the young manager, his face a glow of hope.

With this the others crowd around her with exclamations of such delight and astonishment that Myra feels herself once more a member of the histrionic band and the heroine of the hour.

" When can you get 'em ?" asks Footlights, in a doubtful way. " To-morrow ? "

" TO-NIGHT ! I'll go and see about it now !" And Myra darts away, but is followed by Teddy to the door.

There he sneers after her, with the air of a Vanderbilt : " Bet you a thousand dollars you can't get those uniforms, Myra."

And she cries back to him, in the voice of an Astor : " Bet you a million dollars I can !" then flies down the path, joyous, happy, excited ! If she can't act, she is at least wardrobe-woman. She is one of the company once more !

But coming in sight of her house the child pauses, turns pale, and mutters : " If she finds me out, she'll slaughter me for this," then remarks, with triumph in her youthful eyes : " Footlights said I should be head costume-woman for the Peekskill Opera House and have free admissions. I'll—*I'll do it if ma skins me !* "

CHAPTER III.

FOR two or three days after this, matters run along very smoothly at River View. Mrs. Bushnell, occupied in getting her children ready for their return to school, which begins the coming week, as it is now near the end of September, does not notice that Myra is in an apparent fever of anxious excitement. She has nearly forgotten her daughter's histrionic ambitions, when one day the girl remarks : " I suppose, mother dear, you have no objection to Hettie and I going over to see Footlights's grand performance in ' The Hero of the State Camp.' It comes off to-night—Arthur is super, you know."

" No, I don't think I have any particular objection to your being one of the audience, Myra," replies Effie. Then she laughs, and continues : " ' The Hero of the State Camp ' ! I've seen some of Footlights's placards. Mr. Higgins, I presume, is the military gentleman who adorns the walls and fences of Peekskill ? "

" Yes ; isn't he lovely ? " murmurs Myra, for Footlights had succeeded in obtaining a number of stock lithographs from some travelling company, representing an officer with ferocious mustachios, and had placarded the place with them, modestly announcing at the bottom of each, in large type : " Mr. James Higgins, the young tragedian, in his startling character of *Captain Hotspur Wiggins !* "

" Yes, you and the other children can go," returns Mrs. Bushnell, and sends rapture through Myra's soul for one short fleeting

moment; for, the instant after, her mother continues : "Captain
Heaton is coming up from the city to-da   I've invested a dollar
and a quarter in a box, and we may troll over and see the
renowned Footlights ourselves."

" You—coming—over ? Bought a box ? " gasps Myra, the
room swimming before her eyes.

"Certainly !" smiles her mother.   " Cyril—that is, Captain
Heaton—will enjoy seeing 'The Hero of the State Camp.'   I
rather think, at one time, he perhaps had an idea that he might
have deserved that title himself."

" Oh, mother ! mother !   Don't take Captain Heaton over to-
night," cries Myra, with a pale face and panicky voice.

" Nonsense, Myra, why not ? " asks Mrs. Bushnell, somewhat
astonished.   " There's not going to be anything there you would
not wish *me* to see ? "   Then she says, very suddenly : " Have you
disobeyed me—are *you* taking part in the performance ? "

" No, mamma ! " gasps Myra, and goes quietly out of the room
without another word, for at the thought of her possible disobedience there has come into her mother's face an expression that the
child does not like to see.

Away from her mother the girl's face grows white, and she feels
faint with terror as she mutters to herself : " Going to the performance to-night—ma and Captain Heaton !   Oh, laws ! I'm a goner !"
And from this time on Myra Bushnell suffers all the agonies of a
naughty child, which are as great, perhaps even greater, than those
of an adult criminal.

Mrs. Bushnell, however, sees none of this, being engaged in her
household duties, and in making herself look dainty and pretty for
the visit of the man she is about to marry ; for Cyril Heaton is
coming up that afternoon.   She has invited Mr. Joseph Whiticar, a
lawyer of the town who has been acting as one of the trustees

3

of Mrs. Bushnell's and her children's money under the will of her
late husband, to meet him at dinner; the other trustee being a
certain Abner Smallpage, who is at present taking a vacation in
Europe with his family.

Engrossed in this labor of love, Effie does not notice a pale
and anxious face peep in upon her several times as she stands in
her dressing-room, until she is aroused by a pleading voice saying :
"Oh, ma ! please—*please* don't take Captain Heaton to the performance to-night !"

For Myra has been unable to stand further suspense.

"Why not?" exclaims Mrs. Bushnell, suddenly. "This is the
second time you have asked me not to go. Myra, you have some
reason for this ! What makes you tremble so ?"

"I—I—ain't trembling. Only—only I don't want Captain
Heaton to get his feelings knocked all to flinders at the performance. The comedian gets off awful jokes on militia officers. He
calls them mashers, and says they catch all the foolish girls in
Peekskill with their brass buttons and swell uniforms—that——"

"That's enough, Myra !" interrupts Effie, with a very red face,
these allusions seem so awfully personal to her. "I don't think
I shall take Captain Heaton there !"

Having gained her point, the girl hurries away, crying, "Thank
you, dear mamma !" in such a joyous and happy tone that Mrs.
Bushnell looks after her in astonishment, for Myra's eyes have
regained their brightness and her cheeks their color in an instant.
Out of her mother's sight, the child laughs to herself : "Fixed ma
again ! These novels are making me awful smart. They teach me
how to twist mother round my finger by a new trick every time
—but, oh, my gracious ! it was a close call—I was 'most scared
to death. If she had stuck to taking in the show—wh-e-u-gh !"
And with a long sigh of relief Myra assumes once more the careless

happiness of childhood, and thinks only of the entrancing joys of that night seeing Footlights's grand dramatic pageant.

Left to herself, the arrival of Captain Heaton soon drives everything else from Mrs. Bushnell's mind.

He has brought some pretty presents with him for her children, and these make her happier than if they had been for herself ; she is so anxious for the man she loves to have also the love of her little ones.

So Effie Bushnell gazes at Cyril Heaton, who is a dashing, *distingué*-looking man of about thirty-five, with a firm, truthful face lighted by a pair of honest, hazel eyes, and thinks her cup of happiness full to the brim.

" I've come up for my trunk again," laughs Cyril Heaton, as soon as he has greeted his sweetheart.

" Oh, yes ; the one you've come up so many times expressly to take to New York with you. The one you *always* forget ! " laughs Effie, rather archly.

" Yes—you see," remarks the captain, " I deposited it here *with a purpose.* When I left the State Camp we were not engaged, so I took the liberty of asking you to store the trunk for me—to have an excuse to visit you. But now, that I don't need any excuse, I'll take my trunk back with me to-morrow, as I shall soon have to use its contents."

" Oh, indeed. For what ? " asks Effie, a little curiously.

" Well—I'm going to give a farewell bachelors' dinner——"

" Oh, Cyril ! "

" To the officers of the regiment, and full-dress uniform is the only thing that'll do justice to such an occasion," laughs the captain.

" Ah, I see," returns Effie. " Well, I'll have the trunk brought down from the attic to-morrow morning, so you won't forget it this time. But come into the parlor, Cyril ; Mr. Whiticar is waiting for us and his dinner together ! "

" Whiticar ! Oh, yes ; the trustee for your children's property," returns Cyril. " Well, I hope he won't wait too long _after_ dinner."

To which remark the blushing Effie does not reply, and in another moment they are in her pretty parlor, where they meet Mr. Joseph Whiticar, who has already arrived.

This gentleman is, perhaps, forty, though he looks much older, and has lines in his face that no man's should have till after fifty ; these are, perhaps, the signs of early dissipation, perhaps the results of exhaustive toil ; for he is considered the most hard-working lawyer in Peekskill, and lately to his legal duties has added those of Sunday-school teacher and member of the town-council. For he has recently joined the church, and been elected a member of the city government—the first, to the astonishment of everybody, for there were curious rumors about early youthful dissipations in the recollections of old inhabitants ; the last, to the surprise of no one, for he had always been active in practical politics.

Not content, however, with joining the church, Mr. Whiticar has made himself its most active member ; has practically appointed himself superintendent of the Sunday-school ; and when Deacon Rawson (Teddy Rawson's father) is absent, as he often is, being a pilot of one of the great day-boats to Albany, he passes the plate on Sundays, always being at his post in church.

Perhaps in repentance for youthful transgressions, Mr. Whiticar is extremely jealous, and, like all new converts, most fanatical and illiberal ; for he attributes good meaning to few outside his own denomination, and has Christian charity for, as the village wit remarks, nobody but himself.

As he is introduced to him, Cyril notes that his eyes are never still a moment, and when directed toward him they blink as if they would sooner be looking at anything else.

Mr. Whiticar is bald-headed, and, dressed as he is, in professional broadcloth, in most respects appears the picture of a country lawyer.

The trio dine together, for Mrs. Bushnell does not believe in having guests at her dinner-table disturbed by the precocities of the younger members of her family ; though the children come in to thank Captain Heaton for the pretty presents he has brought them.

This Arthur and Hettie do so frankly and gratefully that Effie's eyes beam with happiness ; but Myra, with her mouth full of Cyril's candy, only says " Thank you " when prompted by her mother, and even while doing it frowns at the captain ; for she looks upon her coming step-father from a dime-novel point of view, and in this class of literature the unfortunate second husbands of mothers with children are always depicted as social monsters who rob unprotected orphans of not only the natural love of their mothers, but also of any property that should be theirs by right of inheritance— these acts of robbery being accompanied by deeds of inhuman cruelty under the guise of parental discipline.

The children, however, do not stay long or say much ; their minds are full of but one thing, and that is the dramatic sensation they are to witness this night—to which they very shortly depart.

After dinner is over, Mrs. Bushnell announces to Mr. Whiticar that she has been particularly anxious for him to meet Captain Heaton, her *fiancé*, as her future husband will necessarily have more or less business with the trustee of her own and her children's estate ; and with these words goes out, leaving the gentlemen to enjoy their cigars together.

While she is saying this, Cyril remarks a peculiar twitching of
Mr. Whiticar's eyes, though that gentleman congratulates him
heartily on his coming marriage, and says he will be always happy
to explain to the captain the investments he has made for Mrs.
Bushnell and her children.

To this Cyril responds that he wishes his future wife to manage
her own fortune ; still, as her husband, she can always command his
advice and business assistance, and after he has married her he
will accept Mr. Whiticar's offer and look over the investments
made for her and her children.

"Very well—after the marriage, then," returns Whiticar, eagerly, and the conversation drifts into general channels. A few
moments later, however, he asks : "When will the wedding take
place ?"

To which Cyril replies, "In about six weeks."

"Six weeks!" says Mr. Whiticar, blowing the cigar-smoke lazily
away ; though if Heaton could see through the table he would
notice the lawyer's lower limbs are trembling as if they had the
palsy. "Six weeks! You young men are always in a hurry."

"So would you be if you were in my place," laughs Cyril.

"Perhaps—perhaps!" and Mr. Whiticar smiles in return,
though his face seems pale in the lamplight. Then he remarks :
"I'm glad it's no sooner—for my co-trustee, Smallpage, will be
back from Europe by that time, and we'll all go over the securities together. Ah! here's Mrs. Bushnell again. I presume you've
been putting the little olive-branches to bed ?"

"By no means!" says Effie. "The olive-branches have all gone
to the theatre."

"My Sabbath-school scholars! To the theatre?" This
comes in such a tone of pious horror from Whiticar that Cyril
smiles and Mrs. Bushnell feels called upon to explain.

IF HEATON COULD SEE THROUGH THE TABLE, HE WOULD NOTICE THE LAWYER'S LIMBS TREM-
BLING AS IF HE HAD THE PALSY.

Which she does, giving them an account of Myra's histrionic ambition to appear as one of the company in Footlights's grand militia spectacle, "The Hero of the State Camp."

"Footlights! That must be the gentleman I saw adorning the walls about the railroad depot. He looked savage enough to be a major-general. I wonder if he wouldn't amuse us! Wouldn't it be just as well to stroll over and increase the young manager's receipts? Rawson's place is next to yours, I believe, Effie?" remarks Cyril.

"I hope you will not think of encouraging such a performance," returns Mr. Whiticar. "The theatre is dissipation for adults, but for children it is perdition!"

This invective only makes Heaton the more eager, for he is anxious to have Mrs. Bushnell all to himself this evening, and thinks from these remarks that the lawyer will certainly refuse to accompany them. He says, shortly: "I don't think we'll come to any harm over there, and Effie will be able to judge whether the effect of the juvenile drama is bad or good upon her children." And rising from his chair, for Cyril Heaton is a man of action, he continues: "Mrs. Bushnell need not wrap up very much; the night is warm and pleasant, and a little walk will do us all good."

But here Effie, remembering what Myra has said to her in the afternoon, astonishes her sweetheart by saying: "Cyril, I think we had better not go."

"Why not?" asks her lover. "Of course, if you have any serious objection, I'll bow at once to it."

"It's hardly so much as that," replies Mrs. Bushnell. "But, Cyril, I'm afraid the performance will wound your feelings as a militia officer."

"My feelings as a militia officer! They're not very sensitive. How will they be wounded?"

To this Effie makes no direct answer. She does not wish to tell him what Myra has said to her about the comedian's jokes. It would be hard to repeat these even were Cyril and she alone ; but in the presence of a third party such an explanation would be exceedingly unpleasant. So she simply says : " Of course, if you wish it, we'll walk over for a few minutes—I happen to have a box." And, leaving her lover wondering why she did not wish him to see the performance, she hurriedly puts on her bonnet and cloak.

" I presume you will hardly countenance the affair by your presence, Mr. Whiticar ?" remarks Heaton, who is delighted at the thought of being left alone with his sweetheart.

" No, I don't think it would be right for me to go, now that I am superintendent of our Sabbath-school," returns the lawyer.

" Ah ! of course not !" says Mrs. Bushnell, who now thinks she will have an opportunity of telling her future husband the purport of the comedian's jokes, unembarrassed by the presence of a third party. With this she takes Cyril's proffered arm, and all three come to the front door and out into the garden.

As they pause to bid Mr. Whiticar good-night, Heaton laughingly says : " I expect we'll see half your Sunday-school over there," pointing toward Rawson's barn, that can be seen above the surrounding shrubbery.

" Half my Sabbath-school at a dramatic performance !" cries the lawyer. " I'll—I'll step over and see for myself. It's my duty to go !" With this Mr. Whiticar places himself upon the other side of Effie as they walk along, giving her no chance for explanation to Cyril.

Upon nearing Rawson's barn, which is illuminated by a number of tallow dips for the occasion, the place is resounding with plaudits, catcalls, whistles, and other demonstrations of juvenile applause, for the curtain has just fallen upon the First Act of " The

Hero of the State Camp," and Mr. Higgins has just bowed his acknowledgments and withdrawn.

The place is now comparatively quiet, and their entrance into Box A makes a little sensation. Teddy's father and mother, as well as a number of their neighbors, are present, having come to witness the efforts of their children.

The adults occupy the more prominent places, but behind them the auditorium is filled by the boys and girls of Peekskill, who are at present killing time between acts by a vigorous mastication of candy, peanuts, and fruit. Prominent among these is Myra, in an apparent state of rapturous excitement, munching an apple. The girl is seated upon an upturned barrel, her face a flush of joy, and her feet beating a tattoo with the orchestra, which consists of three boys—masterly performers on the banjo, the comb, and two pairs of bones.

These are at present operating upon " Marching through Georgia," with doleful effect upon the nerves of the adult portion of the audience, as well as those of Grip, a ferocious bull-dog attached to the Rawson place, who is now howling a staccato accompaniment to the orchestra, that comes into the barn in weird notes as he strains upon his chain, anxious to get at the intruders upon the domain it is his duty to guard.

As Mrs. Bushnell and her party take their seats in the box, Mr. and Mrs. Rawson nod to her, and Myra, who sits behind them on the opposite side of the house, following their gaze, notes her mother and Captain Heaton, and, as she looks, becomes pale and terrified. The flush leaves her face, her teeth chatter as they munch the apple, and her feet no longer beat time to the music, though the little heels of her boots fairly rattle against the side of the barrel, for the child shivers as if she had the ague. The room actually grows dark to her, and her jaw drops.

This is unnoticed by Mrs. Bushnell, who is looking about the place with some curiosity ; but a boy, sitting behind Myra, appreciates a portion of the situation, for he whispers to her : " Hooked it, eh ? Didn't think your mother would come here and catch you ?

You'd better scoot home before she drops on you !"

But Myra is too miserable and frightened to answer ; she simply gazes at her mother, a childish statue of despair and terror. Wild thoughts flit through her brain—oh, if something would happen before the curtain goes up again ; if the place would only happily catch on fire, she wouldn't mind being a little burned or trampled under foot ; if lightning would considerately strike this dramatic temple, she would welcome the thunderbolt with outstretched arms ; or, should a kindly earthquake shake the place into tottering ruins, the rending ground and opening chasms would have no fears for her. She has once read in a dime-novel of a boy holloing " Fire !" to drive his pursuing teacher out of a theatre, and is nerving herself to this desperate expedient ; when, in a second, the little curtain flies up, and in a burst of applause the catastrophe is upon her ; for Footlights, with theatrical sagacity, has reserved a *coup de théâtre* for the second act of his drama.

THE BOYS GREET HIS MARTIAL APPEARANCE WITH YELLS OF DELIGHT.

In the first he had appeared in citizen's clothes ; now the rising curtain discloses him in the full-dress uniform of a captain of the Twenty-second, as he strides out of the sentry-box labelled "General Head Quarters," and defies the villain, Captain Redfern Jinks, to single combat. His military trousers are much too long for him, but he has rolled them up and thrown in an explanatory line, for he remarks : "A rainy day, so, scoundrel, I will not lay you in the dust, but in the mud ! Ha! ha !"

The effect of this is electric. The boys greet his martial appearance with yells of delight, but it also electrifies several in Mrs. Bushnell's box party. Captain Heaton gazes at the boy-actor in speechless astonishment for a moment ; then mutters to himself : "The infernal dramatic scoundrel ! HE'S WEARING MY NEW DRESS UNIFORM !"

CHAPTER IV.

B UT if Footlights's appearance astounds Cyril Heaton, it has even a more potent effect on Mr. Whiticar. After two or three quick glances across the ten feet of space that separates them, the lawyer's face grows pale and frightened. He shrinks back, and from this time on seems to wish only to escape notice. This is not difficult, as candle-illuminating power is not great, and the farther end of the box is dark and gloomy.

Mrs. Bushnell, however, enjoys the efforts of the youthful actors, though she can't help wondering how Footlights succeeded in obtaining such an elaborate and correct costume.

Her thoughts, however, are suddenly disturbed, for at this moment she hears Cyril, at her side, mutter: " The other's stolen Lieutenant Maguire's uniform that was packed with mine."

To this she whispers, " What do you mean ? "

" I mean," says Captain Heaton, " that one of those boys is masquerading in my new uniform, and the other in that of my first lieutenant, both of which were in the trunk I left with you, Effie ! " This last is said slowly and severely, for Cyril has just remembered that Mrs. Bushnell objected to his coming to witness the performance, and for the moment he half suspects she has lent his regimentals for dramatic uses.

It is only for a second, however, for Effie exclaims, suddenly : " Impossible ! The trunk has been in the attic ever since you sent it there ! "

" Nevertheless, that's my uniform ; I'll swear to it ! " returns the captain, who now becomes silent and chews his mustache, gloomily watching the antics of the boys on the stage.

At this Mrs. Bushnell suddenly gives forth a little " Oh ! " and, becoming embarrassed, grows red and pale by turns, for she, too, *remembers*, and is horrified to think that Cyril may suspect her reason for objecting to his visiting the play was that he would recognize his uniform. She mutters, " Those awful children ! " and gazes savagely about for her offspring. Arthur is upon the scene, and as she looks at him her face grows very severe, for the poor little fellow is pale, awkward, and shivering from a tremendous attack of stage-fright that his mother construes into guilt. In the audience she cannot discover Myra, for that young lady has silently departed from the joy of the drama, which now becomes ecstatic to its juvenile witnesses.

For Footlights suddenly fells Teddy to the earth by a right-hander from the shoulder, and Teddy, lying prone upon the stage, challenges him to mortal combat.

To which Mr. Higgins cries, " Ha ! ha ! "

Then the two draw the dress-swords of the captain and his lieutenant, and there takes place the terrible acrobatic sabre-duel in which, as they cut at each other, Footlights throws somersaults between parries, and Mrs. Bushnell cries, under her voice : " Oh, the monsters ! Cyril, they'll ruin your uniforms."

Next the two juvenile actors fight behind the trees, to come on again, for Teddy to die, covered by Tim Jones's real blood. A performance that is by no means to the advantage of his costume, and which makes Heaton glare at the combatants.

This glare is noted by Footlights, and, as stage opportunities present themselves, he glares back at the captain; thinking him an envious swell, jealous of his conquest of some fair lady in the

audience.   These glares of the young tragedian into the box have
such an effect upon Mr. Whiticar that he slinks out of it into the
open air.

THE GRAND ACROBATIC DUEL.

Then, after muttering : ' Does that boy recognize me ?   There's
but one thing for me —I must drive him out of town !" he goes
silently and thoughtfully home to his wife and family.

The lawyer is soon followed by Mrs. Bushnell and Captain

Heaton, for, as soon as the curtain falls on the act, that lady whispers to her escort: "Please come with me, Cyril; I have something to tell you as we walk back!"

So the two go out together, missing the grand concluding dramatic climax in which Footlights, as *Captain Hotspur Wiggins,* is tried by court-martial for the murder of his brother-officer, and only saved by the appearance of *Redfern Jinks's* ghost, who stalks in at the trial, to the comic dismay of the assembled military, as well as his slayer, whose life the spirit saves. For he announces to his quaking listeners that "*Captain Wiggins* butchered him in fair fight, man to man and blade to blade. Ha! ha!" and disappears by the glare of a burning bluelight, as *Captain Wiggins* clasps the woman he has saved to his militia breast as his blushing bride.

As they walk toward her house, Mrs. Bushnell quickly explains to Cyril the reason she had hesitated about taking him to see the performance, telling him of the peculiar appeal Myra had made to her and of her daughter's extraordinary regard for the sensitive feelings of a militia officer.

"Ah! Then Myra is the young lady who borrowed the uniforms?" returns the captain.

"No—I fear it was Arthur, and that she wanted to prevent his being discovered," says Effie. "I am greatly distressed, whoever it was, that anything intrusted to my care by you should have been so treated. You know that, Cyril!"

"Of course. But the affair is nothing but a joke, anyway. How those two young tragedians did go for each other with their dress-swords!" And, seeing that his sweetheart is worried and agitated by the occurrence, he tries to turn the matter into ridicule.

"You may laugh at the injury to your uniform," replies Mrs.

4

Bushnell, "but I do not laugh at the thought that one of my children must have taken articles of value surreptitiously from my house—besides, I feel that I am myself to blame in the matter."

"Oh, nonsense!" cries Heaton. "I won't allow that—what right had I, anyway, to make your home a storage-warehouse? I'll send over to-morrow morning and replevin the uniforms from Mr. Footlights, and any damage to his regimentals I'll fix with Lieutenant Maguire."

"Thank you, Cyril! You are very kind," mutters Effie, giving him a grateful look as she relinquishes his arm; for they are now at the door of her house.

The moment they are inside, Mrs. Bushnell bolts to the garret, having a kind of lingering hope that her lover may be mistaken and the uniforms still be there. A moment's examination shows that the trunk is empty, and she comes down-stairs, to find Captain Heaton still retaining his overcoat and hat.

He remarks: "You look worried, Effie, so I'll say good-night and go down at once to the Eagle Hotel. I shall come to see you again in the morning, and look up my regimentals before I return to New York."

"Won't you stay for a few moments till my children have come home—till I find out who was to blame?" pleads Effie. Then she suddenly cries, "GOOD HEAVENS! MYRA!" and flies up-stairs, for a fearful scream has come from that young lady's room.

The captain rushes up also, but waits outside the door, and, a few moments after, Mrs. Bushnell comes to him with a very serious face, and says: "Cyril, may I ask you to go for my doctor at once? Myra is very ill. She has eaten something that has disagreed with her. She has fearful cramps!"

This is undoubtedly true, for now, through the half-open door, comes to them, mingled with screams and shrieks: "Mother! mother! Oh, how they hurt! Oh, laws! Oh my! Ough! My gracious!"

And Mrs. Bushnell gasps again: "The doctor! *Quick!*"

But here the little girl, who has apparently caught her last words, yells: "I won't have a doctor! Don't send for a doctor. He'll give me medicine! I hate doctors! Ough! Oh, laws! Oh my!" And screams more piercing than before come to their ears.

But, to Heaton's astonishment, Effie seems relieved, and there is almost a smile on her face as she says: "I don't think she is sick at all!"

"Not sick! Then what is she?" asks the captain.

"GUILTY!" whispers the mother. "When Myra has been very bad she always gets the cramps to escape punishment. But I'll investigate a little further. I hear Arthur in the hall. Come with me, and we'll find out if Myra does really need the doctor."

With this Mrs. Bushnell runs down-stairs, followed by Heaton, and, catching Arthur, who has just come in, his face flushed by dramatic triumph, she leads him into the parlor.

The boy is about to eagerly tell her of his exploits, but her serious face stops him as she says: "Arthur, did you take two uniforms out of the trunk in the attic and lend them to Foot-lights?"

"Uniforms? Not much! I wonder where he got such corkers."

"You did not take them?"

"Of course not! Where'd I get such things? Besides, I am a super, not a costumer!" And the boy draws himself up so proudly that the captain stares at him and mutters an astounded "By Jove!"

A moment after, Arthur, who is a philosopher in a childish

way, remarks : " Perhaps this'll tell you what you want, mother,"
and produces from his pocket a crumpled paper, headed :

" PEEKSKILL OPERA HOUSE PROGRAMME."

" Why, I did not get one of these," says Effie.

" No," replies the boy ; "they ran short, we had such a big
house. Footlights got Georgie Sharp, who has a printing-press, to
print them ; but Georgie got tired of printing after a while, so
we didn't have many. But at the bottom you see who furnished
the costumes."

He gives the play-bill to his mother, and after the cast of performers she reads :

"SPECIAL SCENERY BY JAMES HIGGINS, ESQ.

FURNITURE BY THE KINDNESS OF H. RAWSON, ESQ.

CANDLE, BLUE-LIGHT, AND RED-FIRE EFFECTS BY ALEXANDER WARD

AND ASSISTANTS.

PROPERTIES BY TIMOTHY JONES, ESQ.

COSTUMES BY M. BUSHNELL AND ASSISTANTS."

" ' M ' don't stand for Arthur, does it ? " says the boy, with a grin.

" Certainly not," remarks Effie.

" ' M ' stands for Myra," remarks Arthur, "and now she's let
you suspect me. I'm glad I gave her away! Mother, can I get
anything to eat ? " With this the boy strolls off to the butler's
pantry, for the labors of the evening have made him hungry,
leaving Mrs. Bushnell and the captain gazing at each other.

" So it was Myra, as I guessed," says Effie, and then, with a
sigh of relief, " Now I'm certain she is not sick."

" Well, Myra is welcome to the loan of my uniform. You tell
her so for me," replies Heaton, noting a rather set and severe
expression upon the widow's face. " But I must be saying good-
night," and he moves to leave the house.

"Very well," returns Mrs. Bushnell. "I presume it is late, and I have Myra to settle with before I go to bed." She points up-stairs to the chamber of the little girl, which is very quiet now, and accompanies him to her front door to bid him adieu.

"You'll be up to-morrow morning?" remarks Effie.

"Certainly," replies the captain. Then he repeats: "Tell Myra she is welcome to the loan; she didn't mean any harm by it. Sleep over the matter before you speak to her."

"Perhaps you are right, Cyril—I will take your advice, and not talk to her about it till to-morrow." And Effie goes up-stairs thanking Heaven that the man she is about to marry has so much consideration for the follies of her children.

Cyril steps out in the moonlight, happy that, perhaps, he has saved Myra some pangs. After walking down the avenue leading from Mrs. Bushnell's front porch to the main street for a few steps, he pauses in the shelter of an elm-tree to light his cigar.

As he strikes his match he thinks he hears a slight rustle in the shrubbery beside him; he holds up the burning lucifer, and by its faint light imagines he sees an indistinct form creeping away from him. Instinctively he calls out, "Who are you?" and gets a reply that astounds him, for a childish voice says: "I'm Myra, and I hate you, and want you to leave me alone! Mother's sent you out to look for me, I suppose?"

After a moment's pause of surprise, he asks: "What are you doing here?" and receives another shock, for the answer is: "I'm running away from my cruel mother!"

Stifling a laugh—for Cyril has that rare quality of being able to figuratively place himself in other people's shoes, and reflects that what is an amusing incident to him is probably a serious affair to Myra, for the child's voice is full of mingled tears and rage—he says, "And where are you going?"

"Out into the cold—cold, heartless world!" cries Myra, quoting
from one of her dime-novels, in such a heart-broken tone that Cyril
imagines that Effie has really punished her, and inquires : "What
has she done to you?"

"Nothin'; but she's going to!"

"Come back, and see what she *is* going to do to you," says
Cyril, taking the little girl by the hand; but here she astonishes
him again, for she cries: "I won't go back! Don't touch me! Don't
take me back!" and fights him off with all her childish might.

So, finding there is nothing else for him to do, Cyril Heaton
picks up Myra tenderly in his strong arms, and strides back with
her to her mother's house.

This he does despite her screams, tears, kicks, and struggles,
for the child attacks him fiercely and, at one time getting hold of
his mustache, fairly makes him wince. In a few moments he rings
at Mrs. Bushnell's front door, which is instantly thrown open by
Effie, who, with pale face and trembling voice, gasps : "My child!"
for she has just discovered the absence of her loved one.

"She's all right—barring rage and temper!" says Cyril, striding
into the parlor still holding Myra, for the attack on his mustache
has made him rather savage.

Here, by the light of a lamp, Mrs. Bushnell examines the fugi-
tive, who would be a pathetic and woful picture to her mother
were she not so angry with the child. For a little, unfastened shoe
has slipped off one of her feet; her clothes, hastily put on in her
hurried preparations for flight, hang in wild disorder about her
slim, graceful figure, and her cheeks are streaked by dust and tears;
while through her hair, that hangs dishevelled over her face, two
flaming eyes glare out at Captain Heaton, showing that, though
captive, Myra is not conquered.

Assured of the safety of her loved one, Mrs. Bushnell's anger comes to the front. She cries: "You awful child! Why did you get out of bed and sneak down the back stairs out of the house, to frighten me to death?"

"I was going to run away!" cries Myra, defiantly.

"Going to *what?*" gasps Effie, astonishment for a moment conquering displeasure.

"Run away!" repeats Myra. "Run away! Lots of girls run away for less!"

"Why, what have I done to you?" asks Mrs. Bushnell in a trembling voice, for her child's reproaches wound her to the heart.

"You were going to, though!" cries the girl. "For borrowing his uniform. Oh, how I hate him!"

Here Cyril, who has been looking on, sees that for some unaccountable reason the child has grown to dislike him. It is vital to his future happiness that he proves to her he is her friend. He promptly says: "I told your mother, Myra, that you were very welcome to the loan of my uniform!" and would take the child kindly in his arms.

But suspicion is not to be conquered in a moment, and she breaks from him, repeating: "I hate you! Making such a fuss about your miserable old uniforms. Footlights could have hired them for a dollar." Then she stamps her little foot and cries: "Do you think I would stay to be whipped?"

"Whipped?" echoes her mother, astounded.

"Yes! Teddy said if you found out about the uniforms you'd whack me."

"Myra!" says Mrs. Bushnell, with a pale, stern face and a tone in her voice that awes the girl, for she is fearfully angry at the child's unjust attack on the man she loves, "I have never whipped you, but——"

Here Captain Heaton promptly interposes. He knows, if her

mother punishes Myra on account of this night's adventure, she
will attribute it to him, and with childish unreason never forgive
him, and he is desperately anxious to gain the little girl's trust,
friendship, and love.

He says: " Effie, don't say another word, or you'll repent it !
For some reason Myra attributes to me her troubles of to-night.
For my sake, promise me not only to forgive her, but never to
mention it to her again ! "

This has an immediate effect on all ; the child gives him a grateful glance, and the mother returns : " Cyril, you are right—entirely
right. You have saved me saying, perhaps doing, what I would
regret. You are so thoughtful, you make me ashamed of myself. "
Then she takes Myra in her arms, and, giving her a mother's kiss,
says: " Run along to bed. I forgive you, as Captain Heaton
requests, and shall never say another unkind word to you about
to-night."

The child returns the kiss and mutters, " Good-night, dear
mamma ! "

" Good-night, little one ! " cries Cyril.

Then Myra comes to him and offers him her hand ; and would
have given him her heart, for her eyes have a tender look in them,
did not the young man, trying to put things on an easy, off-hand
basis, make a great mistake. He takes the tiny outstretched hand
in his, gives it a friendly squeeze, and, patting the girl kindly
on the head, laughs : " You're all right now, little one ; but, after
this, military discipline, eh, Effie ? " and would kiss the child ; but
she suddenly starts and shrinks from him, then goes sullenly out
of the room and up to bed.

Here she mutters to herself—savagely : " Bossing my mother as
if he was my father already ! Military discipline ! that's what's
ahead of me when he marries her. Military discipline ! I'll find out

— what — that is! Mil-i-ta-ry—" The last syllables are a suc-
cession of sighs as sleep comes upon the little girl and gives her
rest.

"God bless you, Cyril," mutters the mother. "You are more
considerate to my children than I am myself. You have won
Myra's heart as well as mine, I think," and she bids him good-
night once more, with a radiant face.

Then Cyril walks down to the Eagle Hotel, happy in the idea
that he has captured the friendship of his future wife's little girl—
as he would have, but for his two thoughtless words.

Next morning Captain Heaton goes back to New York, having replevined the uniforms from Footlights, but leaving a lot
of trouble for himself and Effie behind him. He has planted a
careless phrase in the child's heart that will bring forth bitter
fruit.

Oh, if the old but reflected that what is a little word to them
is sometimes a great idea when magnified by childish spectacles;
that what is fiction to the wisdom of age is often fact to the inexpe-
rience of youth—then age would be more careful of what it gives
to youthful ears.

.   .   .   .

"Teddy, what is the meaning of military discipline?" asks
Myra the next day.

"Military discipline!" says the boy, slowly. "What's that got
to do with you?"

"It's got a great deal to do with me. That Captain Heaton,
who is going to marry my ma, got her to let me off last night for
borrowing his old uniforms, but he said that after this I should
have military discipline."

"Did he?" remarks Teddy. "Then it was a treacherous trap
of some sort. Step-fathers are always kind to the step-children

till after they catch on to the mother and the boodle, and then
—wheugh!"   The boy gives a long and mysterious whistle.

"But what is military discipline? That's what I want to find
out," repeats Myra.

"Well, I don't exactly know; but you can bet it ain't nice. I'll
see if I can get a pointer on it from one of 'The Wide Awake
Series,'" says Teddy, who consults dime-novels for general information as other people would encyclopædias.

"Will you? That's good," cries Myra. "You find out what
military discipline is, and I'll give you a prime apple."

"Done!" answers the boy, whose weak point is his stomach.
"Make it two big red Kings, and I'll post you straight."

"All right," returns the girl, who is extremely anxious on the
subject. "You'll tell me—when?"

"As soon as I can get on to it. You bring the apples to the
gate at three to-morrow, anyway," remarks Teddy, and he strolls
off to look over the catalogues of his favorite publications.

This he does with such success that at the time appointed he
meets Myra at the little wicket that separates his father's grounds
from those of Mrs. Bushnell.

The little girl cries: "Have you found out what military discipline is?" and holds up the fruit to him.

"Yes!" answers Teddy, and coming to her he remarks, with
some sympathy in his chubby face, for what he has read appalls
even him: "Give me those two apples and I'll post you. My
gracious, Myra, I pity you! You'd better give me all them apples,
for after you've read what's ahead of you, you won't want to eat
anything for a week!"

"Is it so awful as all that?" gasps the little girl, for she can see
that even Teddy is affected, and knows that he is not generally
sympathetic.

"Awful? Just you read that, and shiver! That's what military discipline is!"

With this he places in the child's hands a novelette, entitled "The Drummer Boys of England," a story devoted to the adventures of a lot of unhappy urchins who served in the British Army some fifty years ago, when barbarous flogging was the custom in that service. The book is filled with bad wood-cuts showing the atrocious punishments suffered by the little heroes themselves at the hands of a fiendish drummajor, as well as the tortures they inflicted upon unhappy private soldiers in pursuance of their duties at the triangles.

"MY GRACIOUS, MYRA, I PITY YOU! AFTER YOU'VE READ WHAT'S AHEAD OF YOU, YOU WON'T EAT ANYTHING FOR A WEEK!"

As Myra looks at these she grows very pale, and tremblingly whimpers: "Is — that — military — discipline?"

"You bet! I thought you wouldn't want to eat after seeing those pictures." As Teddy says this, he takes Myra's last apple from her unresisting hand.

Poor Myra is too horrified to care even for apples; she only whispers, with a little, plaintive sigh : " Mother wouldn't let Cap Heaton do such cruel things to me."

" Didn't he boss her last night ? " cries Teddy.

" Yes, but that was when he asked her to let me off."

" Well—will she say no, when he bosses her to put it on ? Ain't she awfully gone on him ? Ain't he playing it deep down ? Isn't he waiting to catch on to your mother and her boodle ? Didn't he laugh and say : ' After this, military discipline '? Did mammie say no THEN ? " urges Teddy, who has had from Myra all the particulars of the interview.

" No ! " mutters the girl, " mother did not say a word." Then she cries out, wildly : " He shan't marry my ma ! I hate him. He shan't be my father ! " and clinches her little fists in impotent rage.

" Come with me, Myra," cries Teddy, with unconcealed triumph in his voice. " I'll show you how to play it lower down than he does. I'll give you a pointer from ' The Servant Gal's Revenge ' that'll knock Cap Heaton silly ! "

CHAPTER V.

"SUSAN, is that all this morning's mail?" asks Effie, two days after the evening of the dramatic representation.

"Yes, mum!" replies the trim serving-maid and trips down-stairs, leaving Mrs. Bushnell alone in her pretty boudoir, as blushing and joyous as any young widow about to contract a second happy marriage.

"Two letters! One from some tradesman, I presume"—with this Effie tosses a rather dirty and very badly addressed envelope to one side of her dressing-table—"and the other—from Cyril!" With this exclamation she tears open the letter from her *fiancé* with a pounce of joy, and devours it with eyes and heart at the same moment. "How nicely he writes! How lovingly he writes!" This last is a sigh of contented happiness; for though Effie Bushnell had loved her first husband as well as any girl can love a man old enough to be her father, she was giving to the coming second one the really great passion of her life. The reading of this love-letter is punctuated with little exclamations of joy, and, after going over it twice—line by line and sentence by sentence—she deposits it in a receptacle devoted to various other treasures of a similar nature and in similar handwriting. Then, putting two or three little finishing touches to an already charming morning-toilet, she turns to leave the room.

As she does so, her eye catches the epistle that she had carelessly discarded a few moments before, and, picking it up daintily for the envelope is somewhat worn and dirty, and the stamp has apparently been mucilaged on by a grimy thumb—she opens it, gives a little laugh, and says: "It looks as if it came from a beggar." With this she picks out of the envelope a piece of paper, evidently a fragment torn from some old account, note, or copy-book, and proceeds to decipher a very badly written letter.

As she does so, her pretty blue eyes stare in horror; the fresh morning blush fades from her cheeks; she gives a gasp, then a horrified, "O-o-oh!" and, sinking overcome on the sofa, wrings her hands and bursts into hysterical tears. For this horrid thing stares her in the face and pierces her heart:

Peekskill September 21st 1880

Honored Mum
I hears with regrets that you are about to fall into the clutches of a military villian— WATCH HIM

There is but one man who can be the "military villian" referred to in this portentous epistle, and that is the man she has promised to marry—Captain Cyril Heaton.

Cyril, though a stock-broker, had been a devoted lover, and had stolen many hours from Wall Street to pass them by the side of his *fiancée* whom love was making to look younger day by day; and the autumn had been a very happy one for Effie till this awful

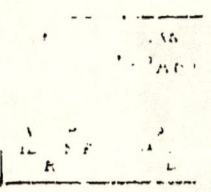

"MYRA, YOU'VE BEE'N READING ONE OF THOSE DIME-NOVELS AGAIN."

morning; but *now!*—now she is writhing upon the sofa, making, notwithstanding her distress, a very charming picture, the morning sunlight of bright autumn coming in through the latticed window and illuminating her graceful figure in her white morning-robe and making her pretty eyes see rainbows in her tears.

This state of partial coma does not last very long. Mrs. Bushnell contrives, after a little, to pull herself together, and ejaculates: "Impossible! Cyril is no villain, though he is a soldier."

Then she picks up the letter that has fallen from her hand, reads it over again, and mutters: " Pshaw! I can't believe wrong of him! I *won't* believe wrong of him! It's a horrible falsehood—anonymous, also! Absurd!" and wipes away her tears.

Just at this time her meditations are broken in upon by Myra's fresh, childish voice crying from the hall: " Mother, ain't you ever coming down to breakfast?"

The door is thrown open; a light, girlish figure flies into the room. " Ma!—are you ever—" here the child pauses and looks suspiciously at her mother, and, catching sight of the letter that has caused Effie so much misery, a knowing look comes into her face. She says: " Why, mamma, you look as if you had been getting it red-hot from some one!"

" Myra! how dare you address me in such awful slang!" cries Mrs. Bushnell, sternly.

" It's not slang, mamma."

" Not slang! Then what is it?"

" It's literature!" remarks Miss Myra, promptly and proudly.

" What?" This is a gasp of astonishment! Then Effie cries, suddenly: " You've disobeyed me! you've been reading one of those dime-novels again!"

" No, mamma!" cries Myra; " it was a paper. I quoted from a

5

serial story in 'The Boys of New York,' entitled 'The Wicked Step-father; or, The Orphans' Boodle.'"

"'The Wicked Step-father; or, The Orphans' Boodle'!" gasps Effie, her thoughts carried by this significant title to the awful letter in her hand.

"Yes," babbles Myra; "it's a tale about a mil—a—a villain who marries a very rich widow and would rob her two beautiful children of their property, were it not for the heroic efforts of the chivalric Knott, the boy-detective. Teddy says it's true, too—that Footlights was an intimate friend of Knott's when he was in New York."

Most of this extraordinary statement is unheard by Mrs. Bushnell, who has gone into a brown-study and is again reading the anonymous letter, unheeding a curious, cunning twinkle that comes into her daughter's eyes as she watches her mother's occupation.

"You can go down-stairs, Myra," murmurs Effie, rousing herself for a moment. "Get your own breakfast, and tell Susan to see that Arthur and Hettie take theirs."

"But *your* breakfast, mother?"

"I—I don't care for any this morning," says Mrs. Bushnell, wearily.

"Mamma, you're not ill?"

"No—but I am busy. I'll—I'll breakfast afterward. Go and tell Susan what I say, *at once!*"

This last stops discussion, and Myra goes out, her brown eyes very wide open and mysterious. In the hall she takes a sneaking peep through the partly open door, and, seeing her mother with a pale and agonized face, she mutters: "She's got it red-hot! I'm —I'm sorry for poor ma, but I won't have a step-father, and Teddy said it would work just as well as it did in 'The Servant Gal's Revenge,' and—I'm hungry."

With these extraordinary words this nice little girl goes down, and, joining her brother and sister, eats a hearty breakfast, unmindful of the misery she has left up-stairs. For the "Orphans' Boodle" has set Mrs. Bushnell's thoughts upon her little ones, and, as she reads the letter over and over again, she mutters : "My children! For their sake, I must let my heart make no mistake! God help us all, if I give my darlings a wicked stepfather!"

A quarter of an hour after this, Myra is cheerily munching away at a plate of batter-cakes, generously covered with maplesirup ; Arthur, her brother, is likewise occupied, and little Hettie has just finished her bread and milk, when Mrs. Bushnell comes into the dining-room with a very serious face, and says, in an awful voice : "Did any one of you children take a postage-stamp from my room yesterday?"

To this question Arthur says nothing, being too much interested in his batter-cakes to reply. Myra, apparently, is equally hungry, and eats convulsively, though an attentive observer would notice that she forgets to place any sirup upon the last mouthful of cakes ; but little Hettie says, cheerfully : "A postage-stamp —a green one, mamma?"

"Yes, my child, a green two-cent stamp. Did you see anything of it—one with a V torn out of the edge of it?"

"Why, that's the one Myra had yesterday!"

At this Myra's batter-cakes seem to choke her, while her mother looks inquiringly at her.

"Myra, did you get a green postage-stamp from my room yesterday, like the one I have described?" says Effie, very seriously. "MYRA!"

This last is a cry, for Myra is apparently choking.

"MYRA! why don't you answer?"

At this Myra gasps out, in a frightened way: " I—I don't remember any postage-stamp."

" Well, you ought to," says Arthur, between mouthfuls, " for I saw you with it myself."

" Oh, yes—I recollect now. I—I—" and the girl seems to be thinking deeply.

" What did you do with it?" inquires Effie, eagerly and impulsively, with perhaps a little suspicion in her voice.

" I—oh, yes, I remember now. I gave it to the poor young woman," cries Myra, suddenly.

" The poor young *woman!* " gasps her mother.

" Yes, one who was inquiring about here and asking for money. I had no money, and your postage-stamp was all I could find to give her. She looked so distressed and pretty, and seemed hungry."

" A woman! My heaven! A *pretty* woman!" mutters Mrs. Bushnell, with quivering lips.

" Why, mamma, you're crying!" lisps little Hettie.

" No, I'm not! Don't talk nonsense, Hettie!" And with these words, said in rather a trembling voice, poor Effie darts from the room, rushes up-stairs, and is heard to lock the door of her chamber behind her, where she goes into a kind of frenzy, and, with jealousy now added to her misery, mutters: "A woman! A *pretty* woman! Oh, Cyril! Cyril!"

As for Myra, she gazes after her mother's retreating form and chuckles to herself: " If I hadn't worked on her the racket I read in the ' Pretty Waiter Gals of Gotham,' she'd have dropped on me." Then, apparently having no further appetite, she goes out of the dining-room into the beautiful grounds that surround the house, and leaves the other two children looking at each other in astonishment.

After a moment Arthur remarks, sententiously : " I don't see why mother makes such a fuss over a miserable two-cent postage-stamp. She must be hard up for ready money," and goes back to his breakfast.

The facts leading to Mrs. Bushnell's curious question have been these. She had hastily made up her mind to write to Captain Heaton to visit her and explain, if he could, the purport of the anonymous letter she had received. After sealing the letter, she had suddenly remembered that she had only a single postage-stamp left ; one that had been in such a dilapidated condition that she had hesitated to place it on a letter, fearing that it would not pass current in the mail. But, the distance to the post-office being considerable and her hurry being great, she had determined to use this stamp and was searching for it, when suddenly, to her aston-ishment, glancing again at the anonymous letter, the identical postage-stamp she was looking for stared her in the face upon the envelope addressed to her. At first she could not believe it pos-sible ; but, not finding the missing stamp, and being perfectly familiar with its appearance, having noticed, a dozen times, that it was torn in a very peculiar manner, she became convinced that the anonymous letter had been mailed her from her own house. Filled with astonishment, Effie Bushnell had instituted the inquiry that had brought misery upon her. The stamp was hers, but had been given by Myra to a woman, a *pretty* woman, lurking about the premises ; begging, perhaps, being merely a pretence to discover the relations that Captain Heaton bore to her. This letter had been written by a woman. Thus jealousy, that all women who love sometimes feel, comes into her heart to torture her.

As for Myra, after walking about the grounds in an aimless, dazed manner (for this unexpected turn in her plot has frightened the girl), she is suddenly roused from her revery by : "Say, Myra, what's the matter with you? Has your mother whacked you?"

These words come from Teddy, who is swinging lazily upon the gate in the hedge that cuts off River View from his father's country-house. As he swings, he contentedly munches an apple.

Myra turns to him and, drawing herself up to make every inch of her four-feet-eight tell, haughtily remarks : "Teddy, I wish you to remember that I'm a young *lady*, and my mother treats me as such. Though, by the howls I heard last night from your barn, I'm sorry to know that your father does not as yet regard you as a man."

With this last parting sarcasm the girl turns away, thinking she has crushed her derider; but Mr. Teddy gives a yell of laughter, and cries : "You heard him, then! That was Bob Savage we were initiating into the band. We initiated him so awful that his shrieks scared my mother nearly to death. She thought somebody was being murdered in the stable."

"In the band! Initiated! What band? Tell me, please." And, curiosity conquering hauteur, Myra, with questioning eyes, turns to Teddy once more.

"Well," remarks the boy, between munches of his King apple, "I thought that would bring you round. You see, since the theatre closed——!"

"The Peekskill Opera House closed?"

"Yes! closed for the season. Tell you about that another time. So we've organized the Peekskill Juvenile Society for the prevention of crime, and call ourselves the Junior Pinkertons. We—that is, Footlights and myself—first thought of organizing as pirates or river-thieves—we could have got a first-class haunt for plunder, spoils, and prisoners on one of them islands up there." And he points up the Hudson to where the beautiful river is just leaving the Highlands and coming round Iona Island. "But Footlights, who is a most practical fellow, suggested that detectives have a much finer time of it, get as much money, and are never put in jail ; and I, after thinking the thing over, became convinced, from 'The Boys of New York' and 'The Old Sleuth Series' that he was about right, and so we concluded to become local Pinkertons ; and if any one commits crime about here, they'd better look out, for we're on to 'em ! "

" But there are no criminals about here," replies Myra.

" No criminals ! What are you ? " says the boy, with an awful, jeering laugh.

" *I !* What do you mean ? " cries Myra.

" Who sent an anonymous letter with a stolen postage-stamp ? " returns Teddy in a fearfully severe voice. " As soon as your mother or Cap Heaton offers a reward, we, the Junior Pinkertons, are going to denounce you, and you are gone ! There is no need of your trying to run away, for we're on your track. You're being *shadowed !* "

At this fearful revelation Myra turns pale, her knees shake under her, and she gasps : " Why, Teddy Rawson, you told me how to do it ! You cut the letter out of 'The Servant Gal's Revenge,' and told me how to copy it and send it with the stolen postage-stamp ! Oh ! how could you ? "

" How could I ? 'Cause there were no criminals about here, and we had to make 'em. It's part of the business of Pinkerton's men to make criminals, and the Junior Pinkertons are up to the standard. Besides ! " here his voice becomes deep and impressive, " you refused once, I believe, to elope with me."

" Yes—but, Teddy, you know I love you. I'll—I'll do it now ! " gasps Myra, with tears in her eyes.

" Too late ! " remarks Teddy. " Of course, you'd like to skip, now your crimes are about to be discovered. But I'll not let you.

I saw you walking home from school with Johnny Timbs, and from that moment you were *doomed!* Do you hear? DOOMED! I made up my mind to have a hold on you, and I've got it. As soon as the reward is offered—Footlights thinks it'll be at least a hundred dollars—I'm going to denounce you to your mother, and perhaps you'll learn that a jealous detective is a pretty bad man to tackle."

"Oh, Teddy! Please don't be a detective," says Myra, trying a despairing but bewitching smile. " I'd like you ever so much more as a cowboy and Indian fighter."

" Not much !" remarks Teddy. " Footlights and I are practical. Footlights, when he was lemonade-boy

" FOOTLIGHTS SAYS HE'LL NEVER BE AN INDIAN FIGHTER
AGAIN."

for the Buffalo Bill show, tried to lick an Indian one day, and he says he'll never be an Indian fighter again. We are detectives now and forever!"

"But, Teddy, you'll spare me?" entreats Myra, with a sinking heart.

"Can't! It's my first case. I must make a record!"

"But, mother! Oh, what will she do? . And then that hateful Cap Heaton'll be my step-father, and—oh, Teddy, spare me! I'll—give you my—my new watch! It cost three dollars!" And Myra sinks upon her knees before this youthful embodiment of justice.

"Don't dare to try and bribe an officer!" cries Teddy. "Myra, you're doomed just as surely as Jonathan Wild doomed Jack Sheppard!" And with these awful words Teddy, having finished his apple, turns away toward another boy approaching along the road, and mutters, "Shadow Number Two!" then gives three sharp, mysterious whistles, each one of which sends a shiver of dread through Myra's trembling form, and leaves her gasping : "Oh! what will mother do to me when I'm denounced? It'll be *military discipline* now!"

CHAPTER VI.

THE GREAT HEAD-CENTER.

TEDDY'S three shrill whistles being answered, he joins the boy coming along the road, and the two exchange various extraordinary grips and signs; then he exclaims, melodramatically and mysteriously: "Password!"

"SHADOW NUMBER TWO, YOU'RE TO KEEP AN EYE ON THE CRIMINAL!"

To which the other answers, in a low voice: "Tracked and shaddered!"

Upon this Teddy remarks to his co-detective, a lank, gawky boy of about fifteen, with a white, shock head of hair, and a vacant, idiotic stare in his countenance: "Bob Savage, Shadow Number Two, you're to keep an eye on the criminal, Myra Bushnell, and see that she doesn't skip!"

"All right, I'm on to her!" returns Shadow Number Two; "but you'd better go and see the Great Head-center—he's looking for you!"

" Is he?" asks Teddy. " Where's Footlights?"

" At the Police Central Station; he's building a dungeon," replies the other, solemnly.

"Crackey! that's gay!" cries Teddy. "I'll go up to the theatre—I mean, the Police Station—and meet him. The patrols are to report there this afternoon. Don't fail to shadow Myra— she's up there groaning on the grass-plot!"

" I've spotted her already," replies the attentive Savage.

" Remember, if she escapes, your punishment will be *terrible!*" And with these suggestive words, Teddy Rawson leaves his subordinate to his duty, and goes by a roundabout path till he comes to what was once the Peekskill Opera House, but is now placarded "CENTRAL POLICE STATION." In front of the entrance stands the figure of Footlights, in the attitude of a crushed tragedian. This he throws off by an effort on seeing the boy, and assumes the air of a chief detective.

To him Teddy advances, and, after giving him several signs and grips, remarks mysteriously : " Password."

" What's the use of that guff with me, Rawson? You know I'm head of the department," growls the other boy, shortly.

" Yes, but we must do things regular—you must give me the password or it would not be detective-like to confide in you."

" Not to *me*—the boss of the force! Are you mu–ti–nous?"

This last is said in such a stern, commanding tone that Teddy gasps : " Of course, it is all right! Footlights, don't jump on me so, and I'll make my report."

" Don't call me Footlights!" mutters the successful actor and manager of a few days ago, with almost a groan. " When I look at that sign I want to be Footlights no more!" and he points to a placard upon the front entrance :

```
 ...............................................
:                                               :
:          PEEKSKILL OPERA HOUSE                :
:                                               :
:               CLOSED                          :
:                                               :
:            FOR THE SEASON.                    :
:                                               :
 ...............................................
```

then goes into such a paroxysm of despair that Teddy is appalled.

After a little, he ventures to whisper : " Have you got on to the track of the fellow that put 'em up to demanding a license ? "

With this the young tragedian cries out, wildly : " Crushed by the world ! Wiped out by society ! Was it the church hit me below the belt, or did some designing villain stab me in the back with a demand for twenty-five dollars ? " and stamps about as if upon the stage.

" Have you got on to him ? " repeats Teddy.

" Have I got on to him ? " echoes Footlights. Then he hisses through his teeth : " No ! But, I'm going to ! That's why I'm head-center. That's why my actors are now policemen. That's why—" Here he suddenly checks himself, choking off the end of the sentence in a groan ; for Footlights does not give Teddy all his secrets.

The peculiar circumstance that had brought about the young manager's despair and the evolution of his dramatic company into a band of detectives was simply this : Mr. Whiticar, the lawyer, had quietly made a few suggestions to the village trustees, with the result that Mr. James Higgins, the manager of the Peekskill Opera

House, had been served with a notice that if he performed again without taking out a theatrical license he would be arrested.

This disaster had come upon the youthful Thespian when he was in the full of his glory.

At his grand production there had chanced to be one of the reporters of the *Highland Democrat.* He had thought Footlights's performance bad enough to write about. This he had done with a plethora of ironical praise and a flow of magnificent adjectives that had charmed the young actor. The Monday after his triumph, with his first press-notice in his hand, and five dollars and seventy-nine cents in his pocket—for the receipts of his crowded house had reached that, to him, enormous sum, not counting a bad nickel and several valuable articles of merchandise in the way of bottles, bags, old lead, etc.—Footlights sat in front of his theatrical barn and dreamt a day-dream of some time being a Bowery manager and running a Bowery theatre.

The sun shone brightly upon him, the birds sang in the trees, as a man strolled up to him.

"Hello, pard!" remarked the great manager to this ordinary, every-day-looking man, for Footlights in his glory was not too haughty nor too proud.

"Hello, yourself! Here's a paper for you!" And the ordinary-looking man gave the manager an official document. As he read it, the birds stopped singing in the trees, and the sun went out of the heavens to Footlights. "Twenty-five dollars!" he gasped; "I'm to pay *twenty-five dollars?*"

"Yes! or we'll put you in jail!"

"Twenty-five dollars, constable! Lord! you'd just as well have ordered me to hire a *real* orchestra!" Then he groaned: "This is the first soft snap I've ever had in this world, and you've busted it!" and staggered into his deserted theatre; where, the

tears coming into his young eyes, he, unused to handkerchief save
for theatrical effect, wiped them away with his drop-curtain. As
the constable turned to go, Footlights, red-eyed and desperate,
ran after him, hissing: "Who's done this sneak trick to me?
Who's busted me in my prime? Who's my hidden, plotting,
kerniving foe?"

"I don't know!" answered the man, and he was glad he didn't,
for, after getting out of Footlights's sight he muttered to himself :
"It was a mean trick, shutting up the boy's theatre! I'm glad I
didn't know who done it, for that juvenile play-actor looked like
he'd done something nasty to him."

That night Footlights became a *real* tragedian. Without an
audience, unsupported by applauding hands, amid the departing
glories of his opera-house, surrounded by what is now useless
scenery, and facing his drop-curtain that will never be rung up
again, he enacted the drama of Despair and Revenge : despair for
bright hopes crushed in the blossom ; revenge upon the man who
had brought about his dramatic ruin.

For Footlights had too much native common-sense not to
be aware that the Village Trustees of Peekskill would scarcely
have thought of demanding a license from him, unless some
one had suggested the idea to them. Who was he? What
reason had he? cogitated the boy—and could arrive at no conclusion.

Teddy, inspired by the lurid logic of the dime-novel, would have
imagined it was some great rival manager like Barnum, Barrett, or
Booth, who was jealous of his success ; but the hard struggle for
existence, and the contact with the stern realities of a great
city, had driven all dime-novel romance from Footlights's brain, if
any had ever existed there. He did not believe in the sensational,
though perfectly willing to use its effects for his own advantage.

At last, after long thought and sleepless meditation, he cried : " I know a scheme to find out ! "

The next day, using the very dime-novel influence he despised, the boy organized the male members of his company of actors into a detective force ! and, from being a theatrical manager, became the Great Head-center of the Pinkerton Juniors.

At first he had great difficulty in leading his associates into the police business. Some of them, headed by Teddy, wanted to become "The Pirates of the Hudson," but Mr. Higgins held up the detective business with these extraordinary arguments :

First, *detectives were never hung or put in prison, even if they did commit crime.*

Second, *they could always demand and obtain the bulk of any plunder that they found in the hands of thieves as hush-money for letting them off.*

Third, *that no detectives were ever licked or downed by anybody; and in court their evidence was always believed, whether they lied or not.*

Fourth, *that all policemen were good men, because they were policemen.*

These statements, that Footlights knew to be general facts from his experience in New York police-courts, tallied with Teddy Rawson's dime-novel reading.

The Peekskill Opera House Company voted, to a boy, to become the Juvenile Society for the Prevention of Crime, and, under the name of The Pinkerton Juniors, keep watch and order in the village —electing James Higgins as their Great Head-center and Edward Rawson as his lieutenant.

After he had sworn in the force with an awful oath of obedience, Footlights, transformed to Police Captain Higgins, strolled out on to the road in front of the Rawson house, and muttered : " Now,

I'll find out who bested me, and get even with him." Then, looking
down at the village below him, he thus apostrophized Peekskill,
uttering this extraordinary sentiment : " BLOW ME, IF I HAVEN'T GOT
THIS WHOLE TOWN IN MY GRIP-SACK !"

And Detective Higgins was nearer right than even he thought
himself.

He felt that, with juvenile detectives in so many households,
who, from the very nature of their oaths of obedience, would report
to him the most treasured secrets of their fathers and mothers and
brothers and sisters ; and, furthermore, having the power to combine the same and compare the doings of one family with another,
that he had a wondrous power over the quiet little place, that
went on in its sleepy mid-day manner, unconscious of the social agi-
tation coming upon it.

Captain James Higgins had organized his police-force the day
Teddy had tempted Myra to send the anonymous letter ; this even
he admitted was good detective business, for it manufactured a
criminal for whose discovery there would probably be offered a
reward. They could immediately clap their hands on the culprit,
and the reward would place the force upon a sound financial basis.

It is this affair upon which Teddy, after Footlights's paroxysm of
despair is over, makes his report.

After listening in silence to that young officer's description of
the little girl-culprit's terror, Captain James Higgins, the Great
Head-center of the Pinkerton Juniors, suddenly mutters : "I'm
not hard enough for this business. I must toughen myself !"

"What do you mean, Head-center ?" asks the younger policeman.

"I mean I'm not hard enough for the part ; I've got too much
heart to be a cop," answers Higgins, clasping his breast theatrically.
" To be a first-class detective needs a fellow that can play it very
low down."

FOOTLIGHTS'S APOSTROPHE TO PEEKSKILL : "BLOW ME, IF I HAVEN'T GOT THIS WHOLE TOWN IN MY GRIP-SACK !"

"I don't catch on," remarks Teddy, with a surprised look.

"Don t yer? Then I'll post you!" goes on Footlights. "You lured Myra Bushnell to do a mean, sneaky act on her mother. That ain't square, is it?"

"No-o," returns Rawson, dubiously.

"You wait till her mother offers a reward for the criminal, then you give Myra away so you can pocket the cash! That ain't straight, is it?"

"No," answers Teddy. "But it's the way all first-class detectives do, isn't it?"

"Yes, I know they do, and that's what I mean when I say that I'm not tough enough for the biz—I must harden myself—and that busted-up show, that theatre closed in the top notch of its success, that's what hardens me till I've got a gizzard instead of a heart, and makes me feel as if I could wring tears of blood out of this 'ere town that's crushed me with a twenty-five-dollar license!" Here Footlights waves his hand over the surrounding country, and then mutters: "I'm toughened! 'Closed for the season,' makes me hard as nails! We'll give Myra Bushnell away as soon as the reward is offered! I don't care if her mother wipes the floor with her. I've no sympathy with criminals, girl or boy, man or woman. I've got the heart of a regulation New York police-inspector now! Look out for me!"

"I'm glad you feel up to your duty," returns Teddy, cheerfully. "How's the dungeon getting on?"

"It's finished, and a corker! It's just as good as the dark cells in Sing Sing!" remarks Footlights, who has regained his equanimity. "Come in and see it." He gives the password to a solemn-faced boy on guard at the door, then leads the way in, and Teddy, following, discovers that the boys, by their leader's directions, have converted part of the cellar under Rawson's barn into a strongbox capable of holding any one not provided with tools, the door of which is secured by a staple and padlock, looking firm enough to give Jack Sheppard himself some trouble to open it.

This inspection is hardly concluded, when they hear the guard up stairs say : " Password ! " and in answer to him a chorus of assorted juvenile voices cries : " Tracked and shaddered ! "

" The patrols are arriving to report ! " remarks Footlights, and he and Teddy hurry up stairs to hear the details that the youthful officers of justice bring in of their first day's detective work at their various homes and firesides : how they have shadowed mothers and fathers, and brothers and sisters, in the interests of social law and order. For Footlights had impressed upon his force that, as it was right that crime should be punished, so it was right that crime should be discovered, and no good boy could do wrong by revealing the secrets of his household in the interests of justice. Consequently the best boys were the most zealous in their work and most suspicious of their parents' actions.

Perhaps it is some thought of this kind that is in Footlights's brain as he ascends to a cracker-box, which he uses as desk, and looks down upon the fresh, youthful faces of his spies and patrols, each ready and eager to deliver up his family's skeleton to law and justice, for the boy sighs to himself : " This is a tough business ! " then mutters : " But it's a trump card, and I've had so few trump cards in my life to play ; " next goes on, savagely : " Why should I pity this town that's crushed me with a twenty-five-dollar license ? I'll make it repent turning a harmless play-actor into a *kerniving* detective—I'll show it the vengeance of a crushed tragedian ! "

With this he, in a firm, commanding, and police voice, says : " The Pinkerton Juniors will now come to order—quit chewing gum, and proceed to business ! "

CHAPTER VII.

THIS announcement is received in silence; each boy tries to assume a wary, watchful, cat-like attitude, and each youthful face struggles to become crafty with detective cunning.

Then Footlights solemnly calls out : "The patrols will make their reports!"

With this every boy in the assemblage holds up his right hand, and a tremendous snapping of thumbs upon digits is heard.

After a moment's pause of surprise, the head-center, in a tone of supreme disgust, remarks : "Do you think this is a school, you chumps, and I'm a teacher? Quit holding up your hands and snapping your fingers! Remember you're policemen, and not school-children, or I'll play teacher and thrash order into you! Take it quiet!"

At this the detectives look surprised and become silent.

"Now, then, Patrol Number One!"

"Here!" shouts the white-headed Tim Jones, the erst-while property-man of the Peekskill Opera House.

"Officer Jones will report last night's spying," replies Footlights, who is delighted, for he sees that nearly every one of his force has something to tell him, and guesses that the story of some one of them must be interesting and perhaps profitable.

"Lieutenant Rawson will act as secretary, and take notices of all revelations; and the boy—I mean, officer—as lets out a single

word of our meeting, will break his oath, and be dungeoned till
he's sick he ever opened his mouth!" continues the head-center,
savagely.

He has turned the matter over in his youthful mind, matured
by struggles for bread, and, being convinced that curiosity as to the
working up of the various crimes that may be discovered is the only
thing that excites the boyish interest in the police-business, and
will hold his detectives together, he has resolved to permit his
officers to report in the presence of the others ; though he knows
the danger of their most exciting criminal secrets becoming no
secrets whatever. He has, however, shrewdly determined, in case
he discovers anything of particular interest to himself, to postpone public investigation till he can find out all about it on his own
private account. Besides, he wisely hopes that the very hearing
of each report by all the other detectives may stimulate some
boyish mind to a suggestion that may be of value, or bring to
some sharp youth's remembrance some fact that would have been
trivial in itself, but, placed with what the other one is telling, may
amount to a great deal.

With these precociously crafty ideas in his head, Footlights
mutters : " Now, then, Patrol Number One, ejaculate !"

Then Officer Jones, who has been stammering from very eagerness, shouts out : " I've struck a cold-blooded murder—I have.
How's that for high ?" Next he rolls his white-eyebrowed eyes
upon the assemblage, who have risen to a boy in excitement, and,
grinning at them, cries proudly : " 'Tain't many 'tectives strike a
cold, clammy assassin at the fust lick. Is it, Cap ?"

" Keep quiet !" shouts Footlights to the horrified and excited
assemblage. " Remember, you're police-officers, and murder and
killing ain't no more to you than it is to doctors. A crime like
this 'ere one is meat for detectives."

OFFICER JONES HORRIFIES THE JUVENILE SOCIETY BY HIS REVELATIONS OF "PIZEN AND ELOPE-
MENT" AT ST. SERAPHIM YOUNG LADIES' ACADEMY.

Here a clammy calmness coming with his words upon each boy, they all sit down, as their Great Head-center continues :

"Now then, hop along agin, Officer Jones ! Keep cool, and slap it out !"

"Well, Cap, you know the furnace in the laundry up at St. Seraphim female school upon the hill is out of repair, and so my mother does some of the extree washing for the gal scholars ; fancy things—lace and muslin dresses and flimsy-cracks that'd get mussed to pieces in the school-laundry. Wall, yesterday ma sent me up to git the wash and bring it down to our house, as usual. As I was bringing the clothes back to mother and had got half-way down the hill, I climbed into the field and sat down under the big elm, as I always do, to look in the pockets of the dresses for candy, chewing-gum, knick-knacks, etc. I'd found a right smart lot of chewing-gum, for gals are all-fired shiftless about such matters, when I come on a couple of pieces of paper written on, in a pocket of one of the muslin dresses. I was about to sling 'em away when, suddenly, Cap"—here he addressed himself to Footlights—" I remembered your words : ' 'Tectives should always keep their eyes skinned— thar's no guessing whar crime may be nailed !' and so I read 'em, and my blood froze——"

With this Jones produces two pieces of paper upon which there are a few lines written in a pretty, school-girl hand, and reads aloud as follows :

" NOTES FOR MY CRIME :

" POISON IS BEST AND MOST SECRET.

" WHAT POISON? ACONITE—IN SMALL DOSES REPEATED. IT CANNOT BE DISCOVERED. IT WILL TAKE SIX DAYS FOR THE TYRANT TO DIE—TIME FOR THE ELOPEMENT. SHALL I KILL HER AT ONCE, OR LET HER LINGER SIX DAYS ? IT WILL SUIT MY PLOT TO LET HER LINGER."

As he finishes the torn paper his hearers are pale and excited ;
but Footlights manages to say : " By crackey ! you've dropped on
a corker—we'll have all our pictures in the *Police Gazette* for this.
What does the other one say ? "

Then Jones reads again from the second scrap of paper :

"OH ! MY CLAUDE, HOW LONG SHALL THIS TYRANT WOMAN KEEP
OUR HANDS ASUNDER, THOUGH OUR HEARTS ARE JOINED—HOW LONG?
HOW LONG ! ONLY TILL SHE DIES—AND THAT WILL BE SOON—SOON,
MY DARLING LOVE—SOON, MY PEERLESS HERO—SOON—ACONITE IS
DEADLY, SWIFT, AND CERTAIN. I HAVE REASONED WITH MY CON-
SCIENCE AND MY GOD, AND BOTH TELL ME IT IS JUST TO SLAY HER,
THAT OUR LOVES MAY LIVE ! "

" Golly ! part of a letter to Claude ! He's her lover and *accomplish.* We must catch on to Claude and shadder him. But,
officer, have you discovered who is the female villain ? " cries out
the head-center.

"You bet ! I'm onto her !" remarks Jones. " After my blood
got to flowing in my veins agin, I examined the dress—it was
a fairly long one—so she's one of the older gals—about seventeen,
perhaps——"

" Just the age to git smashed all to pieces on Claude ! " interjects Footlights.

" Then," continues Tim, " I got to thinking hard, and nailed
her sure—I looked at the name on her wash-list. It was ' Marion
Lawrence.' "

" Marion Lawrence ! Each one of you remember that name.
The name of the criminal ! Mark her ! Shadow her ! Keep your
eyes peeled for her !" remarks Footlights, impressively.

" Marion Lawrence ! the girl with deep blue eyes and long blonde
hair all flowing round her head ! The one who dresses like a crank,
and turns up her nose at boys !" ejaculates Teddy, rather savagely.

" That's natural, when she's so gone on Claude," answers Footlights. " But we must let no personal feelings work agin her.
Anything further to report, Officer Jones?"

" I rather reckon I have," returns the boy addressed. " After
that I took the washing home to mother, and then went back to
St. Seraphim School to see if I could do some more spying, and
struck it rich. I kind of loafed around, till the gals come out for
play, and got my eye on the criminal, through a busted-out knot-
hole in the fence. She got off alone from the rest of the gals.
After a little she walked up to a teacher in the play-ground, and
I guess she must have asked her to let her go out for a walk—
anyway, the teacher opened a gate for her and she walked out
into the trees behind the school. I shaddered her. Not even Old
Sleuth could have been more wary. She walked along, and I could
see she was meditating and plotting her crime, for she was muttering to herself—then I thought I'd wring confession from her, and
I done it!"

" Done it?" shouts Footlights, Teddy, and the rest.

" I—I scared it out of her," continues Jones, proudly. " I
stepped suddenly behind after she'd got among the trees, and
hissed into her ear: ' How's Claude for high?' She gave a yell,
and jumped like a heifer—you can bet she was skeered out of her
boots! After a bit, she got herself together a leetle, looked at me,
and kinder giggled. That sort of riled me, and I says to her:
' You won't laugh long, for I've dropped on what you are doing,'
and I showed her the two papers as evidences of her guilt, and
remarked, sarcastic-like, ' What'll your teacher think of them?'
Then she started, turned pale, and said : ' Don't, for mercy sake,
show them to Sister Mary—she'd give me fits! She'd tear my
treasure from me!' ' You bet she would. She'd give Claude
the bounce,' I goes on. ' I'm going up to give you away, right

now.' Then she began to plead with me and say how tyrannic Sister Mary was, and offered me a quarter if I'd let up on her, and tried to play it sweet on me, and said that no gentleman would betray a lady's secret."

" If you took the quarter, it must be paid into the general fund of the force !" interjects Footlights, holding out his hand.

" No, cap.! I scorned her and her money !" cries the white-headed Jones. " I said she couldn't mash me—by gum ! Then she scared me, for she whispered : ' For mercy, not to show them papers to the teacher ; that her father had sent her to school here to try and break her of the habit.' With that she went off crying, and I stood stiff and cold, looking at a gal criminal of seventeen that was in the *habit of pizening people.* I would have arrested her right then, but the dungeon warn't ready. Do you think we'd better wait till she's finished off her teacher and a reward is offered, or had we better warn Sister Mary not to eat or drink nothin' till further notice ?"

" We'd better wait further developments," remarks Footlights.

" Yes, she's going to let Sister Mary live six days," rejoins Teddy, " so we can make up our minds whether it will pay best to let her poison her teacher first and then jump on to her for the reward ; or to warn her teacher and expose her before the crime is committed."

" I'll promulgate my orders in the case of The *State vs. Marion Lawrence,* for *pizen* and elopement, at the close of the meeting," says the head-center in a voice that stops discussion. " Next, Patrol Number Two."

" He ain't here," says one of the boys.

" Absent from duty !" mutters Footlights, sternly. " That's Officer Try, I believe. When Officer Try makes his appearance, I'll settle with him."

"He's only ten years old," remarks Teddy, apologetically, "and his little sister brought his report in writing; she's waiting outside."

With this he presents the following, upon a piece of Payson, Dunton & Scribner copy-book paper:

Payson, Dunton & Scribner Series, No. 11.

The pen is mightier than the sword.

Tommy Try His REPORT
Mother slaped me Kause I told her if she dident let up on me I'de run her in. I want her rested for Kruelty, to children. I send this by sister Kause I am put to bed.
PORT OF TECTIVE TOMMY TRY

The reading of this is received with shouts of laughter by the detectives present; but Footlights glares them into silence, and orders Lieutenant Rawson to inform Officer Try's sister that his case will be looked into, and suggest that for the present it would be unwise for the youthful policeman to make threats of arresting his mother. Then he directs Patrol Number Three to report.

This is a boy named Gus Robbins, and his father, being clerk to the Board of Village Trustees, the head-center has hopes he will perhaps be able to tell him the name of his enemy who suggested to the board the advisability of collecting a dramatic license, and so ruined the Peekskill Opera House.

In this he is not disappointed. Patrol Number Three has absolutely torn out a leaf from the Town Records, which he now delivers to Footlights.

"Father brought home the trustee-book to write it up last night ; I remembered my instructions, captain, and did my duty," remarks the youthful officer, proudly, on presenting the page.

"You bet you did your duty," remarks Footlights, after reading the following in the minutes of the Village Board :

"On motion of Trustee Whiticar, it was resolved to collect a dramatic license from the manager of the Peekskill Opera House, that being a place of amusement under the law, at which regular prices of admission are charged, and tickets sold to adults."

"Whiticar! why his son is Patrol Number Five !" yells Teddy.

"Ah, a traitor !" cry several of the boys, and Patrol Number Five would be roughly handled did not Footlights interpose, shouting : "Discipline! The officer as acts without orders will be dungeoned !"

This stern speech produces a momentary calm.

Then the head-center continues : "Patrolman Whiticar, what have you to report of your father's goings on ? "

"I've been waiting my turn," replies the boy, a religious-looking youngster of about fourteen, with a solemnly truthful manner. "I'm no traitor, and I'm here to do my best for the law and order of this town; and if my father is a criminal, I shall not shield him. It would not be right, or according to the teachings of our Sabbath-school."

"Then, Patrolman Number Five, let us know your father's doings!" orders the head-center.

"I—I don't think my father thought he was doing wrong in destroying your show," continues the young officer. "I have good evidence he believed he was right."

"Right to bust up the Peekskill Opera House? What evidence have you of that?" asks Footlights, with withering sarcasm in his voice.

"This evidence. When I came home from the performance of 'The Hero of the State Camp,' I found father waiting for me. He —he gave me proof he thought it was wrong," goes on the young detective, with a gasp in his voice and tears of recollection in his eyes. "And after he had got through, he said : 'Ralph, if I catch you going to that place again I'll give you twice as much more next time.' But sometimes I hardly think father is quite right in his head—I'm afraid he's going to commit *suicide !*"

"SUICIDE!" cries Footlights, for the others are too astonished to give vent to their surprise. "What makes you think that? Is he loony?"

"No! but—but I'm sure he is making arrangements to kill himself!" the boy says, slowly and unwillingly.

"That's a crime agin the laws of the State!" remarks the head-center; "they had Steve Brodie, the Brooklyn Bridge jumper, up for it. As a detective, it's your duty to tell all about it—even if he is your dad!"

"I know that," replies young Whiticar ; "that's the reason I'm informing on him now. Please have him arrested before he does it!" and the boy begins to sob.

" All right ! of course we'll act in time," says Footlights, reas-
suringly. " So go on, Patrol Number Five, and tell us all about
it ! "

" Well," answers the young policeman, choking down a sob or
two, " about twelve o'clock the night before last I got hungry and
sneaked down to the pantry to see if I could find something to
eat. I was at work on some cold beef when I heard a noise and
put out the light right smart. It was father coming down-stairs.
I was frightened to death that he had heard me, and come down to
give it to me ; and I jumped behind the door. He didn't pay any
attention to me, but went straight into the dining-room—he
sometimes writes in it when at home—and sat down to work over
some papers. Our pantry is between the kitchen and the dining-
room. The kitchen door was locked on the other side, and I
couldn't get back to bed without going through the dining-room
that father had lighted up ; so I stood shivering, part with fear and
part with cold, and looked at him go on for 'most all night. It was
awful ! After he had read over some documents he got up and
groaned ; then he rolled his eyes 'round as if in pain, throwing his
hands over his head like you do, Footlights, when playing despair
upon the stage. Next he began to swear ; I knew he was out of his
head when he did that, for father never uses bad language."

" What did he say ?" asks Footlights.

" ' D—n Wall Street !' That's what he said," goes on the boy,
solemnly, and cried : ' Curse the brokers ! curse the stage ! curse
the devil that made me do it !' Then he got his head down on the
table, and sobbed till I was scared and would have gone in to
comfort him, if I hadn't known he would have punished me for
being down in the pantry at night.

" After a while he got quieter, and began looking over the
papers again, and groaned out once : ' What a devil she'll think

me!' Then he looked over more papers and got up and put all
of the documents in his breast-pocket but one, which he placed
in his desk, and I heard him sigh, 'That'll take care of my family
after I'm gone.' Then he staggered out of the room like he was
weak in the legs and went to his bedroom ; and I, after I was sure
he was up-stairs, came out of the pantry and thought I'd see what
would take care of mother and us after he had gone, and it was A
LIFE-INSURANCE POLICY FOR TEN THOUSAND DOLLARS. That's why
I know he's going to commit suicide ! That's why I want you to
stop him ! " sobs the boy.

"Calm yourself, officer ! " remarks Footlights. " There are two
theories about your father's case. One is that he's going to kill
himself, and the other is that he's going to try and beat the life-
insurance company. In either case your daddy will be attended
to. I want to see you privately after the meeting—for this I shall
take for my special work-up. Stop crying like a baby and
remember you're a police-officer ! Next, Patrol Number Four !
We omitted him in the excitement of the moment ! "

"That's me ! " cries Teddy. " I was appointed special detective
on the case of Myra Bushnell, juvenile thief and blackmailer.
I've been shadowing her——"

But here Footlights interrupts him, saying : " I've already got
your report, Lieutenant Rawson."

" But I want to tell how I worked it up," goes on Teddy, eager
to let his brother-officers know of his detective craft.

" That'll have to wait till next meeting," cuts in the head-center,
who does not care about the matter becoming too public.

" But I—" interjects his subordinate.

" Silence ! Do you want the black cell, Officer Rawson ? "
cries Footlights, in a voice that awes even Teddy to dumb-
ness.

7

" Now, we'll hear the rest ! "

This he does ; one boy reporting that his father gets drunk every Saturday night ; another, that he has discovered a boat-man, Big Mike, who he thinks is a river-pirate, and will be good fun.

" Yes," remarks the head-center, grimly. " River-pirates are *bully* fun. Police-officers always like to tackle 'em—at a distance. I appoint you, Sammy Sweetzer, to shadder him, and report next meeting—if you're alive."

These and a few other matters are now discussed, in which several of the boys talk of arresting grown-up people, running them in, and locking them up in the dungeon, as if they had the full power of the law to uphold them ; for by this time they have persuaded themselves that they are as real policemen as any officers in the New York force—such is the potency of youthful imaginations. Then, having issued several minor orders, Footlights dismisses his officers with the following speech :

" This 'ere detective movement is going to be the making of this town. Before we got our force in working order Peekskill hardly had one arrest a week ; there hadn't been a murder or felony committed here for over a year : now we'll waken this place up to what a sink of crime it is. We've already caught on to a river-pirate, Big Mike ; a girl blackmailer and sneak-thief, Myra Bushnell ; a suicide, or life-insurance wrecker, Jonas Whiticar ; and a gal poisoner, Marion Lawrence, besides several smaller criminals ; and we've only been in business a day ! If that ain't doing good to Peekskill, I don't know what is ; and, if we don't reform this place, I ain't a prophet. Myra Bushnell's case is in Detective Rawson's hands ; Marion Lawrence, the poisoner, will be looked after by Officer Jones, of whose sagacity and craft we have had this day ample proof; the case of the *State vs. Whitiar*, suicide and insurance beat, will be mine own personal one; I will confer with the unfortunate man's son after this meeting." For Footlights's mind is now running on but one idea, "Why did this man persecute me?"

CHAPTER VIII

AN UNFORTUNATE POLICEMAN.

THE last of his youthful officers having left the station, Foot-lights immediately enters into consultation upon the subject that absorbs him with young Whiticar. He eagerly asks various details about his father's domestic life. "Does your daddy often go to New York City?"

"Quite often," replies the boy; "but he went more last spring and early in the summer, though he's got to going again rather lively now. Sometimes he stays away for two or three days at a time—on business."

"What business?"

"Business about Mrs. Bushnell's trust-fund—he takes care of that, now Mr. Smallpage has gone off to England."

This information does not elucidate matters very greatly. Footlights wonders to himself if old Whiticar is down on him for something he has done to him when in the city. He asks, curiously: "Does your dad ever go to theatres in New York?"

"Theatres? My father!" cries the boy, astonished. "He wouldn't go into one for a thousand dollars. He'd think that he was lost forever and amen!"

"Would he?" remarks the head-center. "I've heard of such people. Reckon I never met him at the theatre—must have been the Wild West or Barnum's. The best church-people think buf-faloes, Injins, and acrobats are more moral than actors and

actresses." Then he goes on : "You say your dad cursed Wall
Street? Did he ever play it down there?"

"Play what?—cards? My father would scorn to touch one.
I've often heard him say that a man who would take a card in his
hand would take a drink, and a man who would take a drink would
do 'most anything bad."

"Say! do you know, I think your daddy must intend to suicide,"
returns Footlights, with a grim smile. "He don't consider this
world good enough for him, and is going out of it."

"Do you think so?" gasps the boy. "You must arrest and
stop him!"

"All right, but I must find out more particulars about your
father before I can act. Where is your dad now?"

"He went down to the city this morning. He'll not be
up till late to-night; he generally gets here by about half-past
eleven."

"Then," remarks Footlights, after a moment's consideration,
"you must let me into your house to-night. I want to see your
daddy, unknown to him, when he gets home."

"But—I—I daren't. He's going to wh—" Here a spasm of
agony shoots through the boy's face, and he cuts the word short
for some unknown reason.

"You must!" returns Footlights, savagely, too intent on his
object to notice the boy very closely. "Officer Whiticar, remember your duty. My orders are that you fix me so I shall see your
father to-night!"

"But I—I can't to-night. My report is not good from school;
he's going to——"

"What has school got to do with police biz?" interrupts the
superior. "Obey me! Find a way for me to get into your house
to-night and see your father!"

" Well, then," goes on the boy, after a pause of thought, " If
you'll take the risk !"

" What's risk to a thorough-bred detective ? "

" All right ; I'll fix it, then.   I'll let you into my bedroom ; you
must take off your clothes and go to bed in my place, and father
when he comes in will wake you up—and——"

" That's settled, then," cuts in Footlights.   " I'll be outside your
house at ten to-night.   Remember the private signal—two whistles.
You come out.   I'll slip in and take your place in bed, and you can
come down and sleep here on my stage—I mean, in my private
office."

" Yes, but you must promise never to let my father know you've
taken my place."

" Not much !   I know my business !"

" For, if father discovered, he'd nearly murder me.   Promise
me, Footlights—promise he shall never know !" cries out the boy,
anxiously.

" I'll keep it dark, on the honor of a cop !" mutters the head-
center, who is thinking deeply.   " At ten, remember !"

" Yes, in the road that passes our house," answers the youngster,
and with a smile on his face and a lighter step and more joyous
eyes than he has had before, this day, he moves away.   As he gets
to the turn in the path he looks round, and, catching sight of the
figure of his commanding officer, he chuckles to himself as if merri-
ment would burst him.

The object of his mirth is, however, pondering too deeply to
notice the boy's sudden laughter.   He is thinking on the subject
that now occupies all his mind : " Why does Lawyer Whiticar want
to down me ? "

These reveries are shortly broken into ; Bob Savage, Shadow
Number Two, comes running to him, dragging by the arm

the unfortunate Myra, who is sobbing as if her heart would break.

After a gasp or two, to recover his lost breath, this stout young policeman says : " Cap., there's a telegram been sent from Mrs. Bushnell, so I arrested the criminal at once. She was so frightened at it, I thought she'd bolt ! Is the dungeon ready ? "

At the word dungeon, Myra gives a scream of terror.

" No, the dungeon is not ready—for *her*," remarks Footlights, looking compassionately at the child, who, he can see, is trembling. Then, after a moment, he continues : " You can leave your prisoner with me—I'll question her. Officer Savage, you'd better go home to your dinner, and don't you forget to bring some of it back for me ! "

" All right, cap.," returns Bob, with whom hunger is more powerful than curiosity. ' You won't mind my sneaking out to you some cold meat ; it's 'most impossible to get off with anything warm ! "

" I'm not particular, when on duty, as regards rations," remarks Footlights. " Only bring it big, and bring it quick ! "

At this command, Bob Savage starts for his home at a jog-trot, leaving the head-center gazing at Myra, who, by this time, has choked down her sobs and is regarding the chief detective with a mixture of awe and trust : awe, for his power over Teddy and the other boys—trust, because he has stood between her and the dungeon.

" Now then, don't be scared, little girl," he says to her in a kindly tone.

" I ain't a little girl ! " returns Myra, scornfully ; " I'm thirteen ! "

" Ah ! old enough to know the nature of your crimes agin the laws and be cheeky." With this, Footlights glares at her so severely that Myra begins to tremble again, and apologetically mutters: "I didn't mean to make you angry, Detective Higgins—I only meant I'm not a baby." Then she cries out, stamping her little foot : "I hate to be called a baby !"

"Well, then, you're old enough to know the nature of an oath," remarks Footlights, who has made up his mind to pump Myra of all information she may have in regard to Mr. Whiticar, the trustee of her and her mother's estate. "You swear to tell the living truth to the questions I'll put to you, and I'll let you off the dungeon."

"I will ; indeed, I will, Detective Higgins !" cries Myra, who has a mortal terror of this mysterious dungeon.

"Then hold up your right hand and swear," returns Footlights in an official tone, "as you hope to dodge a red-hot future, to tell the truth, the whole truth, and nothing but the truth, so help you !"

"Y-e-s !" gasps Myra, very pale and impressed.

"Now look me in the eye and tell me all you knows about Lawyer Whiticar !" says her inquisitor.

"I don't know much about him !"

"Don't try to shield him !"

"I ain't—I don't care for him. When he comes to take dinner at our house, I have to get mine with the other children. I don't care what you do to him. He takes charge of mother's money !"

"Well, what else has he ever done ?"

"He—he gave me some candy one day," says Myra, after profound thought.

"Is that all ?" asks Footlights, disappointedly.

"It was *cheap* candy," continues the little girl, who is desperately anxious to give all the information she can, to appease the detective and avoid the dungeon.

"Ah ! a mean-spirited creature !" snaps out her interrogator. "What else do you know ?"

FOOTLIGHTS NOTICES THE BEAUTY OF THE YOUNG CRIMINAL, AND HIS HEART GROWS SOFTER TO HER CRIMES.

" I——"

" Well, what ?   Quick ! "

" I know he's scared of you ! " gasps out Myra.

" Scared of me ?   Now, we're getting on to it.   What makes you think that ? "

" I saw him at the theatre the last night you played.   He came in with ma and Cap. Heaton ; and as soon as he saw you he started—looked frightened and kind of curled all up.   Then he sneaked into the very back of the box, where you wouldn't see him."

" What else did he do ? "

" I don't know ! "

" Look here, prisoner, answer right off, or down into the dungeon ! "

" Don't !   Spare me ! " screams Myra.   " I—I don't know anything more.   I was frightened of mother seeing me, and I ran home right off.   I was scared about the two uniforms I hooked for you.   You remember, I was wardrobe-woman of the Peekskill Opera House.   I ran home and got into bed.   Then I ran away.   Then Cap. Heaton said : ' After this, military discipline '—and I sent the anonymous letter with the stolen postage-stamp.   Teddy put me up to it.   Mercy !   Don't tell mother.   Let me off, Detective Higgins.   Let me off, and I'll let up on Cap. Heaton.   I'll let him be my step-father.   I'll—I'll——"

Here Myra can say no more, her power of language is gone, her vocal organs are so occupied with sobs.   She grovels at the head-center's feet.

" Here, don't cry so ! " he says, consolingly.   " Git up !   You ain't hurt yit ! " and, after putting Myra on her feet again, he essays to wipe the tear-streaked dirt away from the little girl's face, using a portion of the sleeve of his jacket for this ceremony.

As he does so, Footlights notices the beauty of the young
criminal, and his heart grows softer to her crimes; for even detectives are not always made of such stern stuff as to resist the influence of loveliness and appealing tears together.

He pats her on the back to reassure her, and mutters: "You
ain't caught yet. Keep a stiff upper lip and I'll see you through!"

"Will you, though?" says Myra, a gleam of hope illuminating
her eyes, and giving a little color to her cheeks.

"You bet! What scared you so much about the telegram?"

"O-oh!"

"Stop them tears!"

"Y-c-s."

"What scared you so much?"

"It was to Cap. Heaton. If he offers a reward, Teddy'll
denounce me, and then I'll get military discipline!"

"I'll see that Teddy don't denounce you."

"Not if he offers a whole hundred dollars?"

"Nope! Not even for a—cool—hundred!"

This last is said slowly, and perhaps a little reluctantly, for a
hundred dollars is very tempting to a boy who has an empty
stomach and an empty pocket.

"You will save me?"

"Sure!" Footlights's voice is more decided, for Myra's brown
eyes are looking trustingly into his. A moment after, he continues: "Say, do you know you're quite a nice little girl, even if
you are a criminal."

"And do you know, I think you're a real nice boy, even if you
are a detective, and your face is freckled," remarks Myra, returning
compliment for compliment.

"Yes," assents Footlights; "I don't use Recamier Cream, and
am not at my best—but when I'm in store-clothes I'm a beauty.

Now "—here he becomes official and dignified—" I discharge you on your own recognizance, on this condition, that if anything new turns up about Lawyer Whiticar, you tell it me right off. Myra, go home to your mother, and let me think how I can get square with the man who busted the Peekskill Opera House. Don't stay 'round till any of the force comes back, or they may want me to put you in the dungeon ; they're getting awfully anxious to try the dungeon on some one—SKIP !"

Thus urged, Myra needs no second warning, but flies away as fast as her young limbs can carry her, while Footlights produces a cigarette, and takes a contemplative smoke.

But though he disposes of half a pack of his loved narcotics, they aid him to no further conclusion in the matter of Lawyer Whiticar, save that he must see him face to face, so that he may, if possible, recognize his enemy, and determine why he is down on him.

Consequently, fortified by the cold meal that Bob Savage soon after brings to him, Detective James Higgins makes his appearance at ten o'clock that evening in the road that passes the Whiticar homestead, and gives two low and mysterious whistles, the appointed signal.

After waiting until he begins to shiver, for his seedy clothes are not very effective against the cold of this autumn night, Footlights repeats the signal ; but still gets no answer. There are some lights in the lower windows of the house that indicate the family have not all retired, and, guessing that this may keep young Whiticar from his appointment, he draws into an angle of the building that shelters him from the wind, and awaits developments.

It is difficult to be very patient while suffering the agony of incipient freezing, and the young policeman has just grown tired of shivering, and is about to risk another whistle, when the back door of the house opens, and he can distinguish, by the light inside, the form of Ralph Whiticar as he steals out to keep his rendezvous with him.

The two boys meet in the centre of the road, and, after the usual signs and grips, Footlights whispers, sternly : " Why in thunder did you keep me waiting, Officer Whiticar ? Didn't you hear my signal ? "

" That's where the trouble came in," replies Ralph. " Mother heard you, too, and got nervous. I told her it was the wind whistling ; so she went to bed, and I got a chance to come out. You'd better not take the risk—you'd better go away, father might think you a burglar and shoot you."

" Don't try to scare a policeman from his duty ! " shivers Foot-lights. " Let's get in quick, before I shake my teeth out ! " and would lead the way to the house.

" Hush ! don't talk so loud," whispers Ralph, detaining him. " Don't come in till I've explained everything ; for after we get into the house neither of us must say a word."

" All right," assents the head-center with a shiver ; " only make it quick ! "

" We go in by the kitchen at the back, the way I came out," replies the boy ; " then through the pantry into the dining-room. There's no light there, so you must follow me close and look out for the big arm-chair, and not run against it. From the dining-room we pass into the hall, then up the stairs ; the next one to the top creaks, so you be careful to step over it, for mother's door is right opposite the landing—she's up waiting for father. The next room is dad's dressing-room ; then comes mine. The minute you get there you must go to bed, and I'll sneak out. In the morning, as soon as it is daylight, you must leave the house before any one is up. I wouldn't do this, Footlights, if I didn't think father was going to commit suicide ; and if he is, we must notify the authorities and stop him, and—" here the boy's voice becomes pleading—"you must swear, no matter what happens, you'll never open your mouth and say a word, for if father discovered that I let you take my place, he'd make it red-hot for me!"

"I've sworn that before!" mutters Footlights. "I'll get out of the house, safe enough ; and before morning I'll know whether your dad is going to beat the insurance company or kill himself in good faith. Let's be moving!"

They have gone only a few steps nearer the door when Ralph again lays his hand on the head-center's shoulder and whispers : "Think better of it. Don't go in. My father is an awful stern man. You don't know him!"

"Detectives can ginerally take care of themselves, I reckon," remarks Footlights, debonairly.

"But you don't know how severe he is!"

"Rats!" returns the head-center, sneeringly, and steps confidently into the house.

This cuts short all further warning ; Ralph says no more, but cautiously pilots him through the pantry and dining-room into the hall, then up the steps, along the passage, and into his room.

Though a light can be seen under the door of Mrs. Whiticar's chamber, that lady says no word. Safely arrived at his room, Ralph leads Footlights to his bed, and then to the various other articles of furniture, showing him the location of everything, so Detective Higgins will make no noise by encounters in the dark with unexpected tables, chairs, etc. Next, with a silent grip of the hand, Ralph departs, leaving Footlights alone in the house of his supposed enemy.

As this impresses itself on the boy's mind, he sees himself in imagination sneaking after this Whiticar, who has destroyed his theatrical prospects, and shadowing him down to his library, then discovering him looking over his private papers ; then, in the dead of night, after the scoundrel lawyer has laid his wicked head upon his pillow to dream of new frauds and felonies, possessing himself of the documents that will expose him to the insurance company and send him to prison. As his imagination revels in this grand revenge, Footlights mutters to himself : "That'll teach you to bust my show. Now, Lawyer Whiticar, I'm on to you !" and waits and listens for his coming with the eagerness of an Indian in ambush.

But waiting is weary work, and Footlights, being cold, soon remembers Ralph's instructions, and, throwing off his clothes, gets into the bed, which is much softer, warmer, and more luxurious than the drop-curtain of his unused opera-house, in which he has been wont to roll himself each night.

Thus the boy waits and listens ; but he is so warm and comfortable, he fears he will go to sleep, and so miss his opportunity. After a time he thinks a cigarette may aid him to keep awake ; he gropes his way to his jacket, and, finding a package of these and some matches in his pocket, goes back to bed. Then, lighting one of his beloved narcotics, he remarks, "This detective business is luxurious !" and meditates on revenge.

He has smoked enough of these to fill the room with their penetrating odor when he hears—for the night is very quiet—the up-train from New York run into the Peekskill Depot. Then five minutes of anxious expectation, and the front door of Mr. Whiticar's residence is heard to open and close. The lawyer is at home, it being only a short walk from the station to his house.

Footlights rises from his bed, and carefully opens the door of his room a little, hoping to be able to see and recognize his enemy as he comes up-stairs ; but fails in this, as there is no light in the hall, and Lawyer Whiticar immediately enters his wife's chamber, in which that lady is apparently awaiting him. This is indicated to the listening Footlights by sounds of greeting and conversation that come from this room, though, try as he may, he cannot hear a word or distinguish the voices.

After ten minutes of silent and unrewarded waiting, a horrible thought comes to Detective Higgins, that perhaps the lawyer may go immediately to bed and compel him either to the desperate expedient of entering Whiticar's sleeping apartment to steal what private papers chance may place in his way, or else postpone the affair entirely, and try to recognize him the next morning as he goes down to his office.

The plan of entering the lawyer's chamber by night, after a few moments' consideration, Footlights abandons as being entirely too dangerous. Further meditation, however, is now suddenly interrupted by Mr. Whiticar going down-stairs.

Footlights hears him close the door of his apartment, and the sound of footsteps indicates that the lawyer is unaccompanied. He is, perhaps, going to his dining-room to examine the papers Ralph mentioned in his report. He must be followed. The noise coming from below indicates that the lawyer has left the hall.

Detective Higgins is about to sneak cautiously after him, when the door of Mrs. Whiticar's chamber is suddenly opened, and he hears that lady call: "Joseph, come up-stairs! There is a nasty, curious smell up here—I think it's cigarettes! It seems to come from Ralph's room!"

With a muttered snarl of rage, Footlights hastily closes the door of his lair of safety, and tries to find the key to lock it; but it is not in place, so he hurriedly gets into bed, in order to feign sleep. He hears Mr. Whiticar run up-stairs, where a hurried conversation takes place between him and his wife. This conversation is indistinct at times, but Footlights catches Mrs. Whiticar's voice

8

saying : " It isn't possible, Joseph, that boy can, after the bringing up we have given him, be smoking cigarettes ? But if he is, I will stand no more between you and his correction. I asked you to spare him for his bad school-report ; but now, if he has been guilty of such a habit, do your duty ! "

The next moment there are hurried steps along the hall to the door of his sanct-uary. A masculine voice that makes him start, cries out : " Ralph, you've been smoking ! Come out ! "

To this Footlights, mind-

MRS. WHITICAR : " IF RALPH HAS BEEN SMOKING CIGARETTES, DO YOUR DUTY, JOSEPH ! "

ful of his promise, makes no reply.

Then the same masculine voice is heard in the darkness, very stern and solemn : " Ralph,

FOOTLIGHTS : " THIS DETECTIVE BUSINESS IS LUXURIOUS ! "—PUFF—PUFF.

haven't I told you if I ever caught you smoking I'd punish you so you'd hate the sight of tobacco for life ? "

Footlights still keeps his oath, and gives no answer, save a miserable imitation of a snore.

The next instant the door is thrown open and in his very ear, the voice cries, "Sulking, eh!" And before he knows exactly what has happened, the young policeman finds himself apparently in the grasp of a human steam-winch, the bedclothes are drawn up over the juvenile detective's head and shoulders, there is a horrid swishing sound in the air, and an awful whip, that seems to have been made of red-hot raw-hide, is circling round and cruelly eating into his bare and writhing limbs. Lawyer Whiticar is giving his supposed son Ralph a Solomonic chastisement for smoking cigarettes.

The little bedroom has become a torture-chamber for poor Detective Higgins. In very agony he strives to wriggle from out the bedclothes that are drawn round his head and shoulders; though, mindful of his promise to Ralph, he utters no word as the merciless castigation goes on.

But soon the torment is too potent to be borne by silent flesh; he gets his head out of the bedclothes and utters one awful and hideous yell that brings Mrs. Whiticar to his rescue. She had stood in the hall, listening in sorrow and anguish, her eyes filled with tears at the disobedience and correction of her offspring. This outcry from her supposed darling goes straight to her mother's heart. In an instant she is beside her husband, dragging him from his victim, and crying: "Joseph, forbear! Ralph has had punishment enough. For my sake, spare him!"

Thus entreated Whiticar says, sternly: "That will teach you never to smoke again."

With these words he tosses Footlights upon the bed, where he lies groaning.

The mother says, more tenderly, "Oh, Ralph! give up the awful habit, or you'll break my heart," and is about to kiss her sobbing, fraudulent offspring, when the smoke, of which the little bedroom is still full, overcoming her, she goes into a fit of coughing and so follows her husband to their room.

This has all been done in darkness, and Footlights has as yet never seen the lawyer's face. He lies groaning and writhing on the bed for almost an hour; then, finding the building still, chokes down his agony, cautiously slips on his rags, and carefully and successfully steals from the house.

Getting into the open air, such is the force of habit, he searches for a cigarette, thinking smoke will mitigate his misery. After a momentary investigation of his pockets, he gives a start of disappointment, and mutters: "Curse the luck, I've left 'em all in that bedroom!" Then he shakes his fist at the house and groans: "Lawyer Whiticar, it's double or quits! I ain't seen your face, but your blasted voice I've heard before somewhere! Just let me drop on to that voice, and I'll have you!"

So, with burning limbs, Detective Higgins limps away, thinking, with all the intensity of his youthful mind, "WHERE DID I HEAR THAT VOICE?"

CHAPTER IX.

INSPIRED by this thought, Footlights's sufferings seem easier to bear, and, though groaning and sighing, he rapidly makes his way back to the headquarters of his detective force. Here he is met by Ralph, who has been kept awake partly by unusual surroundings and partly by intense curiosity and terror as to the result of Footlights's visit to his father's house.

The boy says, eagerly: "Did you find out anything?"

"Too much!" answers Detective Higgins, with a suppressed groan.

"What's the matter? You seem to be in pain."

"Pain! I am burning all over! In the darkness, your father nearly flayed me for you!"

"Ha—ah! He larruped *you* because *my* school-report was not up to the standard," mutters the boy.

"No! you can bless your stars," replies Footlights, grimly; "he whipped me for what I done myself. If he had walloped me for any of your cuttings up, and I thought you had put up the job on me, I would knock you out, right here! He whipped me for smoking cigarettes in your bed. Oh! how he laid me out; your dad's an awful strong man. Ough! it was tough, I tell you. Stop your infernal chuckling or I'll massacree you!" For at this tale of woe Ralph has been unable to conceal a snicker.

"D-di-d you give me away to father?" asks the boy, tremblingly.

"No! I stuck to my oath."

"God bless you!"

"Now," remarks Footlights, after a pause of thought, "you must go right up to the house, take your place in bed again, and appear as if you had nearly had the life thrashed out of you. It's the only chance of your dad's not discovering that some one has been in your place; for no living boy could go about natural after the lambasting I got, and if you do not turn up in the morning as if you were a cripple and paralyzed, and had had rheumatic fever and were covered with boils and blisters, he will know that *you* never got the whipping he gave *me*."

"You do not think he has discovered that you have left?"

"No!" says Footlights. "They were all asleep and quiet when I sneaked out of the house."

"Then you did not discover anything about father's actions. Is he going to suicide or not?" asks Ralph, anxiously.

"Yes, I did; I discovered one main thing, and that is, no man who is going to commit suicide would ever have taken the trouble to give the larruping to a boy that your father gave me. Your father's going to make a raid on the insurance company, or something—he's not going to kill himself at present. And, between you and me, I know your father."

"Know my father?"

"Yes, we've been chums some time or other!"

"Chums? Impossible! You saw his face?"

"No, but I heard his voice, and it's as familiar to me as if I had lived with it; but I can't catch on to it yet. You go right straight home, and get into bed as quick as possible, and then your dad will never guess that the boy he whipped to-night was not Ralph Whiticar, but Jem Higgins. Get out quick, and report what you hear in the morning; and remember to bring back my

half-pack of cigarettes that I left in your room !" continues Footlights, the chastisement he has received apparently having had no
beneficial effect upon his love for narcotics.

"All right!" says Ralph; "I'm not anxious to stay here.
That drop-curtain of yours doesn't make a good blanket, and the
rats have a nasty way of running round and keeping one awake.
I'll let you know what turns up in the morning." With this the
boy departs, in so hurried but so cheerful a manner, that Footlights growls after him : "Don't you give me away to the boys, or
I'll make you wish you had stayed and took the licking !"

Thus warned, Ralph hurries home, where Providence is preparing a surprising reception for him.

Filled with sympathy for her unfortunate offspring, and thinking that by this time the horrid cigarette smoke must have entirely
disappeared from her son's bedchamber, Mrs. Whiticar cautiously
leaves the couch upon which her husband is quietly sleeping, a few
minutes after Footlights's flight from the scene of his castigation,
and enters the chamber where the suffering culprit is supposed to
lie.

A moment after, she hurriedly returns to her husband and
awakens him, crying wildly : " Joseph, Ralph has run away !"

"Run away ? I doubt that," says Whiticar as yet half asleep.

" Yes, our cruelty has driven him from home ! I know it !"

" How do you know it ? "

" He has left his room, and taken his clothes with him."

" What clothes ? All his clothes ? "

" I don't know. Go and look for yourself—quick ! He has
surely run away !"

Thus entreated, Lawyer Whiticar hastily gets up and goes to
his son's room, and, finding the boy gone, lights up the house and
proceeds to make a thorough investigation of the premises. In

his search he finds a little article that makes him utter a cry of
astonishment and collapse overcome upon a chair.

While this is going on, Ralph approaches the house, and, seeing it illuminated, knows that his absence must have been discovered. Fearing detection in some way, and not daring to face his
father, he sneaks cautiously to the barn, and goes to bed among
the hay.

The consequence is that Lawyer Whiticar leaves on the morning train for New York, carrying with him in his pocket something
that makes him shiver whenever he looks at it.

As the train rolls into the Grand Central Depot, he mutters to
himself: " This only hurries the matter. It's bound to come out
soon, anyway ; but I must see who's on my track. It can't be Captain Heaton, the man who is going to marry Mrs. Bushnell. My
heaven ! if he suspects me *too soon !* "

With this he goes at once to a private detective office on
Broadway, and has an interview with its manager, which results in
one of their agents taking the first train to Peekskill.

Then Joseph Whiticar goes to his office and resumes the business routine of his daily life ; but every now and again he takes
from his pocket a half-filled package of cigarettes, wrapped in an
old theatre programme. The cigarettes do not appear to excite
his emotions, but the theatre programme does. It is an old worn-
out play-bill of " Martin's " Theatre on the Bowery. Its date is
that of some months back, in the latter part of May. Upon it is
written, or rather scrawled, in his own handwriting :

" Won't you even listen to me when I show you my appreciation of your art by jewels
as well as flowers ? "

Each time his eye rests on this he grows pale and mutters suppressed curses, and cries : " Can that scoundrel boy have played
me false then as he is doing now ? "

As for the youth who has caused these peculiar actions on the part of Mr. Whiticar, he lies all that day groaning and writhing upon his theatre-curtain blanket, disguising the cause of his torment from the members of his police-force, who come to report to him their various exploits in pursuit of crime, by attributing his indisposition to a severe attack of rheumatism, complicated by boils of enormous size and tenderness.

He is evidently too sick to give advice or counsel, though it is desperately needed by his officers, for their detective duties have not been going on over prosperously.

Notwithstanding his sufferings he contrives, however, to listen to Ralph Whiticar when that young officer tells him of his finding his house illuminated upon his return to it the preceding night; of his concealing himself in the barn until his father departed in the morning for New York; of the joy with which his mother received him when he had ventured home for breakfast; and that he, compelled to keep up the deception, had to solemnly swear never to smoke another cigarette in his life, which was easy, as he hated the sight of them.

"Under that showing," remarks Footlights, "you won't feel bad in handing over the half-package I left in your room," holding out his hand for the same.

"I couldn't find 'em," returns Ralph. "I looked for them, but they were gone."

"I reckon your ma must have thrown 'em away, then," mutters Detective Higgins. "A woman would have no idea of the value of such things. She'd never guess they cost five cents a pack."

"No, mother didn't touch them. I asked her about them. I—I said they were borrowed. I had to tell a lie, and I never told one before--not in my whole life. I don't like this business, it compels untruth," rejoins the boy.

"That's so! Detectives have to best criminals with their own weapons. That's part of the business," says the head-center, contemplatively. "Think what a grand thing it'll be for your father, if you keep him from becoming a swindler. How he will bless you for it in after-life."

"Yes, I know that," mutters Ralph ; "but I'm getting afraid he won't be grateful to me in the present if he discovers——"

"You leave that to me! Your dad'll never guess who kept him straight; he'll think it is the law and me. I ain't afraid to tell your dad I did it —if there's two or three officers about to hold him. You skip, and report to-morrow morning what happens at your house to-night!"

The next morning, however, the fortunes of the band are in such woful plight that Footlights is compelled, though still weak, sore, and miserable, to attend to business.

The reports that come in warn him that, if he has any detective force left in another day or two, their exploits will make the peaceful village of Peekskill rise up to annihilate them, for no criminals could ever have produced such uneasiness and excitement as these youthful officers of justice

His first report is from Teddy ; that young detective appears excited but dejected. He has heard rumors that a reward has been offered for the party or parties who have sent Mrs. Effie Bushnell an anonymous letter.

The advertisement, he believes, has appeared in the *Highland Democrat.* He has not seen the paper as yet, not having the cash to purchase one, but understands that one hundred dollars has been offered by that lady for information of the writer. He's pretty sure of that, having seen Captain Heaton at the widow's house the day before. If it is so, he'll soon be in funds.

"This comes lucky," Officer Rawson remarks, "as we'll have to move the headquarters of the force to-day."

"Move the headquarters! Why?" cries the head-center, becoming interested at once, as the headquarters means his office, and that is his sleeping apartment, dining-room, and home.

"Why? Because dad says he's going to be back from Albany to-morrow morning, and if he finds a boy of us on the premises he'll toss him over the fence."

"What makes him down on us—we ain't investigated him?" growls Footlights, savagely.

"Well—I was a little previous, I'm afraid," remarks Teddy, in a shamefaced way.

"Previous! How?"

"Well, you know Hiram Thomas watched the lodge-meeting last night, and he reported that it broke up at ten o'clock. I met him on the street, and he reported the fact; and this morning at breakfast ma said: 'That was a long session of your lodge last night, father?' and he replied: 'Awful long; we had to initiate half a dozen new members.' And I—I——"

"Well—you—what did you say?" queries Footlights, sternly, of his hesitating subordinate.

"I—said: 'It wa'n't *very* late. Hi Thomas, my Junior Detective, said you were all out by ten o'clock sharp, and——'"

"Well?"

"Then dad uttered an awful word, and ma said: 'Why, father, you did not get home till twelve o'clock, and said lodge was just out,' and with that burst into tears. And then——"

"Yes!"

"Dad he jumped for me, but missed me, and I got out of the door and scooted; but he yelled after me: 'I've been wondering what deviltry you boys have been up to. It's detectives you are!

When I come back, if I catch a boy of the gang 'round here I'll do him up—and I'll see you, Teddy, when I return—make yourself happy with that!' "

"Well, are you making yourself happy?" asks Footlights grimly.

"No, and I ain't trying to," mutters Teddy; "but if I get hold of that hundred dollars father won't see me till I've spent it. I'll go off and try to borrow a paper." Then he departs, leaving the head-center very savage at his subordinate's indiscretion, which threatens to leave him houseless.

His feelings are not improved by the arrival of little Detective Officer Sammy Sweetzer, the boy who had reported Big Mike, an athletic Irish boatman of over six feet in stature, as a river-pirate, and had been ironically told by Footlights to take his case in hand.

Officer Sweetzer has taken his superior at his word, and arrives with a tale of harrowing nautical woe.

"I took your orders, head-center," the boy says, stilling a sob into a sigh, "and shadowed Wild Mike last night. He'd been at that little saloon near the landing; he has the reputation of being very hot-headed, but I hardly thought he'd have the audacity to run against the law. As he was getting into his boat, I saw something in the craft that looked suspicious. I said, 'What have you there, my man?' 'Eggs,' he answered; 'I'm takin' 'em to my mother at Jones's Point, where she keeps a boarding-house for the section-hands on the West Shore road. Do you want a row, sonny? Take you over and back with me for a quarter.'

"'That's too thin,' said I; 'hand out your basket till I examine it.'

"'What are you giving me, you brat?'

"'I'll show you what I'm giving you,' cried I. 'Do you know you're talking to a Government detective officer?'

" ' Whirrah ! *you*—a Government detective ? ' he screamed, dropping his oars, and falling on to a seat as if overcome; he seemed weak and convulsed.

" I thought the word ' detective ' had scared him, and jumped

LITTLE OFFICER SWEETZER, OF THE RIVER POLICE, HAS A BAD TIME ARRESTING "WILD MIKE."

into his boat. 'Hold up your hands !' I cried, very stern ; ' I'll take you in and lock you up !'

" Then, for the first time, I was near enough to see that he was laughing. ' By the infant Moses !' he giggled, 'what are we coming to ?'

" ' You're coming to prison,' I hissed in his ear, and, stepping forward to seize him, I plumped into his basket. As they crunched under my feet, I discovered they were eggs.

"Then he got crazy—he'd been drinking, and that made him savage and desperate, but I never thought he'd have the cheek to tackle a detective——"

"But he did, though?" chuckles Footlights, whose own misfortunes have made him unsympathetic.

"Didn't he? 'Ye've smashed my mother's eggs. Bad cess to you!' he yelled.

"'Hold up your hands,' I commanded, and he did hold up his hands; and, after tossing me all over the boat, he tossed me into the water, and as I swam ashore he yelled after me he'd have the law on me for them eggs. Now I want you and the other officers to come down and help me arrest him."

"We can't now, we're too busy on more important work," replies the head-center, struggling to conceal a grin. "We'll tackle Wild Mike perhaps to-morrow."

"To-morrow, sure," returns young Detective Sweetzer. "I'll lie low till to-morrow, for Mike swore he'd smack me every time he saw me. What's the penalty for resisting an officer, anyway?"

"About forty-five or fifty years, I reckon," says Footlights. Then he remarks, sarcastically: "Will that be enough?"

"Yes, that'll even me," mutters the boy, "for the licking mother gave me when I got home last night for playing near the water and getting my clothes wet. I've got to go to school now, but we'll all go down and arrest Mike to-morrow, sure, head-center!"

"Sure!" mutters Footlights, as he gazes after the disappearing form of his misguided but zealous officer—adding to it, mentally, "If we're not all in jail ourselves;" for he knows, after a few more such adventures, the parents of his youthful force will doubtless begin to be heard in the matter.

But misfortunes never come singly. Detective Sammy Sweetzer has hardly gone when Detective Tim Jones makes his appearance, and says, hurriedly : " Cap., I need protection in the pursuit of my duty ! I've just warned Sister Mary of the St. Seraphim Academy that she's to be murdered by slow pizen, and Marion Lawrence, the gal criminal's father's in town, and after me with horsewhip and pistol."

" You must make a full report of the case, Officer Jones, if you wish me to act intelligently in the matter," says Footlights, assuming his most official form of speech; for he knows a sensation or scandal in the St. Seraphim School will soon become the talk of the town, and wishes to ascertain how far the white-headed Jones has compromised any secrecy of action on his part in the cause he has taken to his heart of hearts—that of the detection of and vengeance upon Lawyer Whiticar, the man who has destroyed his first paying enterprise, *i.e.*, The Peekskill Opera House.

" Wall, then, cap., I'll tell it all official," answers Jones, transferring his chewing-gum from one side of his mouth to the other with a smack, as he sits down upon an old box, and, producing an old and worn-out pocket-book, proceeds to make his statement.

" Two days ago, cap.," he begins, " I made my first telling of my dropping on the gal pizening her teacher, from the notes and letters I found in her wash."

" I know all about that—go on !" mutters Footlights, impatiently.

" Wall, then, you give the case into my hands, telling me to shadder her cautious and act judicial. So I loafed 'round St. Seraphim School all day working up the case. I ain't been able to catch on to the Claude her letters spoke of her being in love with ; but I got on to other matters that I reckoned would hang her.

"Next morning I was moving around agin, when mother came down with some knick-knacks to wash, and mentioned incidental that Sister Mary, the head mistress, was sick.   As soon as I heard this, I knew that the Lawrence gal had begun her divilment, and Sister Mary was being done to death.   That was yesterday, and you was too sick to give me p'ints; so I turned the matter first to one side of my brain and then to the t'other, and calculated that if I didn't do something quick Sister Mary would be a goner.   So I writ this anonymous note—I've taken a copy for official filing."

Here Detective Jones produces the following :

PEEKSKILL, *September* 29, 1887.

SISTER MARY MADELINE,
    Head Mistress of St. Seraphim Academy :
    I've writ this to tell you that you are done secretly and silently to death. *Fear every one !* Your illness is proof you are being PIZENED. Don't dare to taste food or swaller drink til further notice. For the prescent I can't tell my name, but indict myself.

THE SILENT DITECTIVE.

"This was given to Sister Mary yesterday afternoon ; since then she's been much worse."

"Undoubtedly," chuckles Footlights.

"This morning she sent for the doctor ; then I knew I must git in my work quick, or, between the pizen and the doc., Sister Mary would be an inquest before night.   As letters didn't do no good, I settled I'd have to try parsonal warning to save the teacher from the pizen of the pupil.

"Ma's doing extree washing for the school helped me.   She was going to carry some back ; I fixed it so I took it for her, and, instead of waiting at the door, I stalked with it right into the kitchen, and said I had a message from mother for Sister Mary.

"'Well, what is it, Tim?' said the cook.

" ' It is something I must give to her direct.'

" ' Oh, it is, indeed!' snaps she. ' Then you'll take it right up to the matron's room—you'll have to trust her with it if you don't me—Sister Mary isn't very well.'

" I didn't wait another invite. I'm powerful cute, I am. Up-stairs I goes, straight to Sister Mary's room, and knocks at the door. Then I stood a-waiting, my heart a-going like a thrashing-machine. I reckon I made up my mind to bolt ten times in ten seconds; but then I recollected Sister Mary had been kind to my mother, and that I ought to save her, and remembered I was a detective, and had the law behind me to back me up, so I stiffened and staid. Then I heard, ' Come in,' in a sweet, pleasant voice, and in I pops, bold as a policeman.

" Sister Mary was sitting up in an arm-chair, looking as if she had a headache, and who does I see with her but the gal criminal herself?

" She was jist saying, ' I'm sorry you're not so well this morning, Sister Mary.'

" When I heard this, I longed to down the hypercritical fiend, and I chipped in, sarcastic-like, ' I reckon not!'

" Then that Marion Lawrence turned, quick as a flash, and see'd me, and I knowed she war guilty, for she got all pale about the lips and cheeks.

" Sister Mary she sat up sudden, looked astonished-like, and said : ' Boy, how did you get in, and what do you want here?'

" ' To save your life!' says I. ' You got my letter last night —you didn't obey my warning—you eat something?'

" ' I thought it was from some crazy person,' Sister Mary replied ' I——'

" ' Ah, then you *did* eat!' cries I. ' That's the reason you've got such a head on you this morning—IT'S THE PIZEN !'

9

" At this Sister Mary gave a little gasp, and the Lawrence gal said : ' The creature is crazy. Shall I go down-stairs and send for a policeman ? '

" ' Don't take the trouble,' says I. ' *I'm one!* and you can't sneak off in that way. I want you, my gal, for pizen and elopement.'

" At this she got as red as fire, and says : ' You miserable fool, what do you dare insinuate ? '

" ' Only what I've got the documents to prove ! ' cries I, pulling out of my pocket the Lawrence gal's two letters.

" When she saw these, the criminal gave a little gulp, and Sister Mary, who had looked on as if dazed, said suddenly : ' What is the meaning of this most curious scene ? Explain, Marion ! '

" Then I chipped in : ' She daren't explain ; but I will. That gal is slowly pizening you in order to get you out of the way, so she can slope with her lover Claude.'

" At this the gal criminal gives such a wild scream of hysterical laughter that she can't stand up, and sinks down on a chair with tears in her eyes, while Sister Mary says : ' Your story is impossible—you don't know what you're saying.'

" ' Don't I ? ' says I, kinder riled at the woman, whose life I was trying to save, turning on me. ' I'd have you know that I am a detective from the Central Station, detailed to work up this 'ere case, by Captain James Higgins, and can prove what I charge— that that creature is a pizener and eloper ! '

" I had worked myself up into such a commanding streak that I 'most scared Sister Mary, who looked at me quite solemn. But the Lawrence gal, who had been biting her lip and giggling, and turning white and red, suddenly cried out : ' *You* a detective from the Central Office ? You're the boy that brings the extra washing every week ! ' With that Sister Mary turns her glasses on me and says, ' I remember you also now.'

"I WANT YOU, MY GAL, FOR PIZEN AND ELOPEMENT!"

"But here a right cute idea struck me. I says: 'Kerrect; I have acted as wash-boy. It war a disguise to work up this 'ere case.'

"'Oh, that was it?' mutters Sister Mary, while the Lawrence gal got red, then suddenly blurted out, 'You're not going to listen to him and read his papers?'

"'Only to prove your innocence, my child!' says Sister Mary. 'Of course, I know it's a mistake.' Then she gives a little start, and cries, sharply: 'Marion, you're not afraid for me to investigate this matter?'

"To this the Lawrence gal answers nothing, though I could see, under her blue uniform skirt, her little foot a-patting the carpet like the treadle of a sewing-machine.

"So I chipped in myself and started to prove my case, just as Old Sleuth does in his series of five-cent novels. 'Can you deny that you visited Gripus & Lint's 'pothecary-store syruptitiously, unknown to your teachers?' cries I, consulting my note-book ; 'fust, on the evening of Sep. 26th at 7 P.M., and on the night of Sep. 28th at 7.30 post meridian!'

"When I mentioned the drug-store racket the criminal gal grew deathly sallow about the gills, uttered a little 'O–oh!' and covered her face with her hands, while Sister Mary looked startled-like and said, very severely: 'Marion, is it possible you left the school-grounds without permission?'

"I could see I was making a good impress on the teacher, and rubbed it in. 'What did you buy at that 'ere 'pothecary-store? If it warn't pizen, what was it? Dare you tell?' says I, tapping my note-book and looking mysterious, like the picture of 'The Silent Detective.'

"She didn't answer, and I went on : 'Can you deny them letters writ in your own hand, that say you're mashed on Claude, and

going to take off your teacher by a-co-ni-tee so you can slope with
the object of your love? Still silent?' says I, very sarcastic-like,
and hands the papers over to Sister Mary, who suddenly cries :
' Marion, this *is* your writing ! '

"'You bet !' says I. ' Didn't she 'most beg me on her knees
for them papers ?' Then I goes on : ' If you says the word I'll take
her down to our jail right now, and lock her in the dungeon.'

" But here Sister Mary suddenly cries : ' By no means ! I've
listened to you because I saw, and still see, that there is something
that needs explanation ; not, Marion, that I believe you guilty for a
single moment of any such absurd crime as you are charged with.'
Then she goes on, and turning to the criminal, commands : ' Did
you visit the drug-store as he describes ?'

" ' Yes,' says the Lawrence gal, suddenly ; " and I might just as
well end this farce and be expelled now as any other time. I did
visit the drug-store.'

" ' With what purpose ?'

" ' To—to buy——'

" ' What? I insist on knowing !' orders Sister Mary, who is
now looking as strict as any school-marm in the country.

" ' To—to buy—' here the gal gets powerful red, and kinder
gasps out—' to buy cigarettes !'

" ' CIGARETTES !' yells her teacher. ' Oh, what will become of
my school ?' and sinks down more horrified than if she had said
pizen.

" ' Yes,' cries the gal, desperately, back at her ; 'cigarettes ! I,
like most other Bohemians, smoke *cigarettes !* '

" ' BOHEMIANS !' echoes the school-marm.

" ' Yes, writers ! *littéralaters !* The papers that idiot has shown
you are notes for my next novel, " The Hidden Sin," that I hope
to have published in the *National Flag*, that never charges young

authors for putting their works before the public. My father has tried to break me of the habit, which he says is making me cranky and strong-minded. And now I suppose you'll expel me—not for writing novels, but for smoking cigarettes. I prefer to be expelled, as I don't like confinement and bread and water. My father is coming to visit me to-day. He'll give me an awful lecture and take me away at once; but as for this wash-boy-detective!'—here she turned on me and gave me the glance of a fiend—' my father won't leave a whole bone in his body for accusing me of *pizen and elopement.*'

"Then I heerd the front door open and a man's voice below. That Lawrence gal cried, suddenly, ' My father! I'll tell him now!' and ran out of the room, leaving me and Sister Mary a-gazing at each other.

"Just then the cook put her head into the room and said: ' Tim, your mother's below looking for you! Why have you been so long?'

"' His mother!' gasps Sister Mary. ' Why, he said he was a detective, disguised as Mother Jones's wash-boy.'

"' Faith, thin, he's been disguised ever since he was born!' cries the cook, with a hideous guffaw.

"Just then I heerd screams from the school-gals below, and an awful man's voice crying : ' The scoundrel's up-stairs, is he, Marion ? I'll horsewhip him and make him publicly beg your pardon!'

"Then Sister Mary gave a yell, ' Oh, the scandal! It will ruin my school'—and mother, down below, cried, ' What's that villain Tim been doing?' And there were female yells and school-gal shrieks all over, and I—I heerd the gal criminal's dad coming up two steps at a time—and then, cap., I—I disgraced the force—I FORGOT I WAR A DETECTIVE, AND RUN AWAY."

CHAPTER X.

"DID I disgrace the force very bad?" mutters the white-eye-browed Officer Jones, after a pause, during which Foot-lights falls upon the floor convulsed with laughter; but sudden contact with hard boards reminds him of his own recent woful police-experience, and he jumps up again with a shiver of present anguish and painful remembrance.

"It ain't kind of you, cap.," returns his subordinate sadly, "to make fun of one of your officers' misfortunes when he comes to demand protection!"

"Who shall I protect you from?" growls the head-center—"the Lawrence girl's daddy or your own mother?" As he says this he glances out of the door, and suddenly whispers: "Tim, she's coming now!"

"Who? Mother?"

"Yes—with a club."

The boy does not wait for more accurate information, but disappears by the back door of the barn, leaving Footlights to confront Mrs. Jones, who is a woman of masculine appearance and most serious demeanor.

"Where is he?" cries she, sharply.

"Whom seek you, madam?" returns Footlights, giving her a quotation from a play, and thinking to overawe her with a dramatic bow.

"Madam!" yells she, very savagely; "don't you dare call me a

madam! I'd have you know that my name is Jones! And who
are you, who calls me a madam?"

"Woman," replies the head-center, "about here I am known
as James Higgins, once called Footlights——"

"Ah! then you're the villain I've been looking after! Furst,
with the dram-mah, you led my poor boy away, and, after making
the crazy fool think he was an actor, you've finished him up by
making him a lunatic and a detective. His cranks have lost me
the washing of St. Seraphim School—stole the bread out of his
mother's mouth—and *you* call *me* a WOMAN!"

At the thought of this last terrible insult, Mrs. Jones raises
her club, and would take vengeance upon the dismayed captain of
the force, did she not fortunately catch sight just at this moment
of her own offspring making round the building to get the start of
his mother in a race down the path for the front gate. "Tim," she
cries, in her sweetest tones, "come here! Darling, don't be afraid
of yer mammy!"

But Tim rather hastens his pace at this beguilement. Noting
his movements, Mother Jones screams: "Ye won't come here;
then I'll go to ye, and beat sinse into ye!" and pursues the rapidly
disappearing Officer Jones down the path.

Despite the misfortunes of his followers, which threaten to
involve him, Mr. Footlights yields to the enjoyment youthful
minds always feel in a well-contested race, and cheers alternately
Tim and his mother as they sprint for the front gate.

His full cry suddenly stops, however, as he sees little Ralph
Whiticar make his appearance on the scene. This youth is evidently much excited; he doesn't even stop to watch the efforts of
Tim to escape his mother—a sight that would, at any other time,
have drawn his instant and enraptured attention—but, dodging
them both, comes running up to Footlights and gasps out, partly

from want of breath and partly from fear: " Head-center, there's
another detective on our track ! "

"*Another* detective ! What are you giving me ? We're the
only detectives in town ! " answers Footlights, confidently.

" But this is a grown-up detective—a man-detective ! "

" A *man*-detective ! A *grown-up* detective ! A REAL detective ! "
gasps Higgins, turning pale, for though he has inculcated in the
youthful minds of his disciples that they are officers of the law,
he has never for an instant deluded himself with that idea.

" Yes ! a grown-up detective," repeats Ralph.

" How do you know that ? "

" Because he came 'round and kinder questioned me. He got
quite familiar with me, talking about things and asking incidental
questions, and treating me to candy ; and two or three times he
playfully slapped me on the back, and I forgot to wince, or yell, or
squirm, and when he kinder laughed and said : ' 'Twa'n't a very
hard thrashing your father gave you for smoking cigarettes, eh,
Ralph ? ' And then I heard him asking the boys if any other boy
had been taken suddenly sick around here the day before, and
Sammy Sweetzer said you had suddenly been struck down by rheumatism, and had boils all over your back, and couldn't lie down."

" Sammy Sweetzer told him that—and what did he do ? " mutters Footlights, his face growing awful to look on.

" Oh, nothing ! He only grinned and talked 'round with the
boys, and Sammy Sweetzer told him we were detectives, and
were going to arrest Wild Mike to-morrow ; then he treated to
soda-water, and Sammy posted him on the point that you were
our captain and inspector. Why, what's the matter with you, Footlights—are you going crazy ? "

This last is said in a tone of horror, for the head-center has
suddenly begun to dance about wildly, crying : " Pile it on ! Heap

it up! Keep the pot a-biling with bad news!" and various other expressions of disgusted agony. After a moment, however, he forces himself to calmness, and says : "What did the detective do next?"

"Nothing."

"Nothing?"

"No; just then the rumor got about the town of Detective Jones trying to arrest the girl-poisoner at St. Seraphim School, and I think he went up that way to see if he could spy out anything about that affair."

Here Footlights suddenly astonishes Ralph, for he says: "That'll give me an hour or two more." Then he adds to the boy's wonder, for he continues : "That detective has been put on your track by your daddy, Ralph."

"What makes you guess that?"

"Guess that! I'm certain of it! or else how did that man, who had never seen you before, know that your daddy, in the dead of night, larruped you for smoking cigarettes? Your father told him. Don't you forget that!"

"My father'll discover that I placed you in my bed. Oh! what shall I do?" cries Ralph.

"Do? Go home and get your lunch as quick as you can, and bring it here to me, for I ain't had no breakfast, and I'll think how to fix things for both of us," remarks Footlights, who imagines that he'll have plenty to do this afternoon, and doesn't care about doing it on an empty stomach. "Don't forget, if you have cold meat, that I like mustard and pickles, and want it quick!"

As Ralph hurries off to do his bidding, luck or fate or Providence produces another surprise for the head-center. Teddy walks in and astounds him by proudly fluttering a hundred dollars in bills in his face.

" Great Scott ! where did you get all that money ?" he ejaculates.

" That's the reward for denouncing Myra for sending the anonymous letter."

" You mean sneak ! " cries Higgins. " You gave the poor
little girl away ! "

" Yes," returns Rawson ; " as soon as the reward was offered,
I did my duty as a detective. I proved it on her, and her
mother's blubbering and sobbing as if her heart would break—
I don't see what she offered a reward for, if she didn't want to
know."

" And she gave you the reward ? "

" No—Cap. Heaton ! After I'd told my tale, he took me outside the house, put the money in my hand, and said : ' There's
your hundred, you miserable, sneaking boy ; but if you open your
mouth to any living being about poor Myra's foolish, childish
prank, I'll make you as sorry as this money makes you glad ! '
Ain't that Cap. Heaton an ungrateful cuss ? " And, winding up
his story with this comment, Teddy begins to count the bills once
more, slowly and lovingly.

" Give me that money ! "

" *What ?* " This is a yell of surprise.

" Give me that money ! " The tone is that of command.

" Well, I did intend to give you some—a little, Footlights, as
your advice helped in the job. You're pretty hard up and you
need a suit of clothes mighty bad, and I don't mind giving a tenner——"

" *Give me all that money !* " This last is said with a ferocious
determination that startles Teddy.

" I—I'll—I'll even go a twenty ! " he mutters, turning pale.

" GIVE ME EVERY DOLLAR OF THAT MONEY ! " and with a sudden

TEDDY APPEARS AT THE ENTRANCE WITH A LARGE PEBBLE IN HIS HAND, WHICH HE HURLS WITH
THE PRECISION AND FORCE OF A BASE-BALL PLAYER.

spring Footlights is on the astounded Teddy, and wresting from him the roll of bills.

The struggle is short, quick, and decisive. Teddy fights with all his little might, but his boyish muscles are as naught to the brawn of a street Arab that has been exercised in the fight for bread upon the thoroughfares of New York, and trained in numerous battles with the bootblacks and newsboys of the Bowery. In an instant Footlights finds himself in possession of the money, as well as several bruises from the fists of his youthful foe. He holds the bills up in triumph.

"So you are going to take 'em all, you thief!" cries Teddy.

"Not one dollar!"

"What do you mean?"

"I mean to take 'em all back to Cap. Heaton—I mean to tell Myra's mother how we roped the child into doing a mean act, and how you scared her about 'military discipline.'"

"You shan't give it back. It's my boodle, you—you footpad!" yells Rawson; "but I'll make you sick of stealing from me!"

With this threat he runs from the barn by the back door. Footlights gazes after him with a melancholy chuckle, which is turned into a grin of dismay as a masculine voice whispers in his ear and strikes terror to him. It says: "Hand me that money, you young thief. I'm the detective sent up from New York to look after your gang!" and a great, powerful man has Footlights by the collar.

With the instinct born of the Bowery, Mr. Higgins pops the bills in his pocket, leaving both his hands free for the struggle, and with the agility of a wiry cat wriggles from the detective's grasp, being aided to this feat by the rottenness of his coat-collar, part of which he leaves in his opponent's hand. Then he turns and makes

a bolt for the back door, fortunately for himself stumbling over a
board before he reaches it ; for at this moment Teddy appears at
the entrance with a large pebble in his hand, which he hurls at his
head with the precision and force of a base-ball player, crying,
" Take that, you ruffian ! "

As Footlights falls, this stone whizzes over his head and smites
the pursuing detective full in the jaw, with a cruel, sickening crunch.
Had it struck his forehead it would have probably stunned the
man ; now it fills him with an awful, cruel passion that must have
its revenge—on something ! His assailant is not to his hand, for,
on seeing what he has done, Teddy has fled with a yell of terror ;
so now the man, with his eyes full of bull-dog passion, his mouth
bleeding, and two front teeth knocked down his throat, to stimulate
his unreasoning rage, falls on the boy who has not injured him as
he rises from the floor, and stuns him with murderous blows upon
the head from his great, brawny fists.

The instinct of self-preservation now comes to Footlights's aid.
Bewildered as the attack makes him, he knows the man means murder, and instinctively protects the back of his head with his hands
as he rushes wildly from the door of the barn. Then, careless of
what course he takes, so long as it keeps him out of reach of that
thing behind him that is landing pile-driver blows upon his burning
head, he flies through the shrubbery.

This course, fortunately, takes him straight for Mrs. Bushnell's
villa ; so it comes to pass that that lady, searching for Myra, who
has been missing since morning, sees a boy, with bleeding face and
torn and ragged clothes, forced by an awful blow through the
pretty hedge that separates her place from the Rawson grounds,
and then stagger along her lawn, pursued by a man whose arm is
raised as if to repeat the attack.

The boy falls almost fainting at her door-step ; the man's fist is

again about to descend upon him, when Mrs. Bushnell, her pretty
eyes ablaze, stands between him and his victim.

"You brute!" she cries. "Don't you dare! Do you hear me?
Don't you dare!" and the eyes of the lady, full of indignant fire,
force the eyes of the bull-dog to droop before hers.

It is perhaps as well for him that they do, for at this moment
Cyril Heaton's athletic form issues from the house, and, calling,
"Effie, what's that man been doing?" the captain of the Twenty-
second stands beside his sweetheart.

As he does so, Footlights gazes up into his face and astonishes
him. He faintly mutters, "I've brought back the reward to you,
Cap.," and presses into his hand the roll of bills.

In answer to Cyril's question, Mrs. Bushnell simply tells what
she has seen.

"Why, you ain't going to stand between me and that young
thief," says the man, who has concluded that further violence won't
do just at present.

"What has he stolen?" asks Captain Heaton, curtly.

"Why—why, that roll of bills he just gave you. I caught him
with the swag—he and another young ruffian in that barn over
yonder."

"You are mistaken," returns Cyril, examining the greenbacks.
"This money he handed me was paid by me for a service; these
are the very bills I used. I recognize them!"

"Well, then, I want the young jail-bird for assault and battery.
Look at my mouth!" and the man places his hand on Footlights's
collar and drags him to his feet.

At this the boy whimpers: "Don't let him get me. He'll murder me, 'cause Ted Rawson mashed him with a rock," then struggles faintly to get away.

Just here Mrs. Bushnell, who has been eying him, suddenly

10

cries out : " Why, it's Footlights, the boy who wore your uniform at the theatricals. You remember, Cyril ? "

" Yes, I remember," says the captain, grimly.

" I'll take care of him," mutters the man, and would drag his victim away ; but the boy whimpers : " If he does, he'll murder me ! " and Effie cries : " Cyril, don't let him ! I saw him strike Footlights."

Thus appealed to Captain Heaton says, sternly : " Let the child alone ! "

" Don't you stand in the way of an officer making an arrest," answers the man, savagely.

" An officer ? Not one of the policemen here ! There are only two, and I know them both."

" No, I am a detective," says the man, as if to overpower them with his title.

At this Mrs. Bushnell, a little awed, stands back ; but Cyril, who has seen such gentry before, returns : " One of Byrnes's men, I presume ? "

" No, one of Glover's ! "

" Ah, a private detective ! Have you a warrant for the boy's arrest ? "

" No ! don't need any."

" I beg your pardon, you do ! You are violating the law by placing your hand on this boy. You have no more authority to make arrests than I have. You've no right to trespass on these grounds ! Get out of that gate ! "

" I'll show the power of an officer ! "

" You're no officer ! Get out of that gate, or I'll show you the power of my arm ! I think I'd better send for one of the local policemen, and have you jailed for assaulting this boy ! They have a jail in the town, I presume ? "

" Yes, I've got one—under the barn," whispers Footlights, eagerly.

"Well, you needn't talk so rough to me—ain't I going?" says the detective.

"Then go—quick!" cries the captain, and the man slinks out of the gate cursing to himself, and muttering: "I'd better see Lawyer Whiticar, and get a warrant."

As for Footlights, he looks on as one dazed, and then whispers to Mrs. Bush-

MINISTERING HANDS, THAT ARE LAYING UP FOR HER TREASURES ON EARTH AS WELL AS IN HEAVEN.

nell, with white lips: "My eyes! ain't he prime? The cap's
downed a real detective!" and begins to laugh faintly; but the
laughter suddenly stops, and he sinks down in a dead faint at
the feet of the lady, who gives a cry of fright, then stoops over
him, and with tender words and ministering hands, that are laying
up for her treasures on earth as well as in heaven, revives this poor
waif of the streets to life and gratitude once more.

After a little, the boy opens his eyes. Noting this sign of con-
sciousness, Effie calls to the captain, who has been assisting her
efforts: "Cyril, get some water! That will refresh him!"

But Footlights mutters, faintly: "No water! I've lived on
water all day. Give me victuals; I ain't tasted none since yesterday."

"Starving!" cries Mrs. Bushnell, her eyes filled with tears.
"Cyril, please carry him into the kitchen." And at her words the
stalwart captain, unheeding his fine raiment, picks up this mass of
rags, dirt, and hunger, and carries it into the house, where it is
made strong and happy and human again, by reviving food, cleans-
ing soap and water, and some clean old clothes that are much too
large for it, but effective as a protection from cold and rain.

With the advent of luxury and comfort, Footlights becomes
himself once more, though his head still aches from the detective's
blows. He beams pleasantly on his benefactress, and astonishes
her—for he says, "Now I am ready for Lawyer Whiticar and his
detective agin!"

"Mr. Whiticar and his detective? What do you mean?" These
are questions from Effie and Cyril, both speaking together.

"I mean this," replies Jemmy Higgins, "that Whiticar knows
I'm getting on to him, and sent that man up from New York to
try and down me, and he would; I'd have been a stiff by this time if
you hadn't saved me and pulled me through, Mrs. Bushnell—and I

ain't going to forget it. I was coming over here to give back the money and to let you into the secret of Myra's being down on Cap. Heaton, when he tackled me ; but I'd best begin at the first."

With this he gives the history of his theatrical speculation : how it was destroyed by a license being demanded ; how he had organized his company into what he had made them think a detective force, in order that he might, through their aid, discover who was his enemy ; how Teddy had worked on Myra's fears as to "military discipline," and instigated the child to send the anonymous letter, copied from the "Servant Gal's Revenge," and sent with a stolen postage-stamp, as related in that extraordinary dime-novel.

At this Mrs. Bushnell says : "Thank heaven ! my darling little girl was not so deceitful as her actions might have made me think her !"

Cyril, however, looks serious and suggests : "This Whiticar is the trustee for your and your children's property ! You say he has not given you your last month's interest—I wonder what the man can fear from Footlights ! "

"You question the boy," returns Mrs. Bushnell, "while I go and look for Myra—I haven't seen her for several hours. Mr. Whiticar, however, promised that my dividends would be paid to me to-day."

With this she passes from the room in pursuit of her absent little girl, while Captain Heaton questions Jemmy as to his relations and discoveries in regard to the lawyer.

The information he receives is not very satisfactory, as Footlights never saw Whiticar's face, and can only say that his voice was as familiar as the tuning of an orchestra.

The captain receives this remark contemplatively, and after a moment or two suggests: " I presume, after what has happened, you intend to leave Peekskill ? "

"Yes," returns Footlights ; " the exploits of my detective force haven't made us popular about here. It's a mighty dangerous thing for small boys to get into big boots—I reckon I'll take the next train to New York."

" Without any money ?" says the captain, smilingly.

" Oh, that's easy enough ! My dad's a station-hand down there at the depot, and i'm pretty popular with the railroad boys on this road ; they'll let me run through on the baggage-car without bothering me."

" And after you get to New York, do you suppose the restaurants would also make you a dead-head ? "

" No, but the theatres will," says Footlights proudly. " I can always get my living about the theatres. There's always something to eat in New York—and it's a mighty queer day when I can't get hold of some of it ! "

" Anyway, you had better take part of this money that you have returned," remarks the captain, passing over to the boy a twenty-dollar bill.

" No, thank you, Cap.," replies Footlights ; " I ain't done nothing to earn this."

" Very well, accept it as a loan—it is much easier travelling with money than without it."

" Right you are ! " mutters Footlights, with a smile. Then he cries out, enthusiastically : " I'll borrow your money, captain, and give you my note for it, for you make me proud ! You're the first man that ever insinuated that I had credit ; and I am told that's 'most as good as capital. Now I has proof of it ! Besides, I'm out of cigarettes, and I don't think the newsboy on the train would trust me for a packet, even if the New York Central did give me a free pass."

At this moment they are suddenly interrupted by Mrs. Bushnell coming hurriedly into the room, and saying: "Cyril, I can't find Myra anywhere. What can have become of her?"

"If she knew she was going to be denounced, you can bet she's skipped!" remarks Footlights.

"Skipped?"

"Yes, run away!"

"Run away? I must find her. Come and help me!" cries Effie, and would fly from the room, but at this moment a servant comes in, and, handing her a document, says, "A telegram for Mrs. Bushnell!"

"Perhaps about Myra!" whispers her mother, tearing open the message. As she examines it her face grows very white, and she ejaculates: "My heaven! my children! what shall we do?"

"What has happened to Myra?" cries the captain, suddenly.

"Nothing that I know of," mutters Mrs. Bushnell, with pale lips. "But this telegram says that Mr. Whiticar committed suicide to-day, by drowning himself at Coney Island; and that it is rumored that defalcation and embezzlement were the causes of his taking his life. Cyril, if this is so, my children and I are beggars! I cannot"—here she pauses and falters—"I cannot place the burden of the support of my little ones upon you. It—it would not be right!"

But here, in her misery, a great joy comes to this woman, for it tells her that she has loved not only well, but wisely; for Cyril Heaton cries out: "Do not dare talk to me in that way—you make me blush with shame! Do you suppose, Effie, that I would not do even more for you, the woman I love, when you are poor, than I would for you when you are rich? Do not fear for your own future or that of your children; only trust yourself, and them, to me and to my love !" And he takes her into his arms, where she breaks out sobbing, though her tears are not all of misery.

Here this pretty little love-scene is rudely broken in upon. Footlights, whose presence they have forgotten, cries out, suddenly, " Did they find the body ?"

" The body ! Whose body ?" answers the captain, while Effie springs from his arms.

" Why, Whiticar's body, to be sure ! If they didn't find the corpse, you can bet there ain't no suicide, and he's trying to beat the insurance company !" yells Higgins, almost beside himself with excitement.

" This telegram does not state," mutters Mrs. Bushnell, after looking over the message.

" Then if they ain't got the body, I'll find the beat !" And with these astounding words Footlights bolts from the room, leaving Cyril and Effie gazing at each other amazed.

" I'll telegraph and find out if they have found the body," says the captain after a moment. " There may be something in the boy's suggestion." For he remembers what Footlights had told him of his discoveries in the Whiticar family.

As for Mr. Higgins, he has become suddenly filled with a great idea. He slinks cautiously down to the railroad depot, for he is mightily afraid of the detective seizing him *en route;* boards the baggage-car on the New York Central train that leaves Peekskill at 5.30 P.M., and beats his way to New York, arriving at the Forty-second Street Depot at seven in the evening.

All the way down he has been turning over the Whiticar affair in his mind. He even steals a read of an extra evening paper from the newsboy on the train ; but that says nothing about the body—only gives an account of the lawyer drowning himself at Coney Island on the morning of the day of its issue.

"TAKE ME TO A PLACE WHERE THEY HIRE ACTRESSES. I WANT TO BE A CHILD-STAR!"

It is dark, and as he leaves the depot he has still the one idea in his mind, " Have they found the body ? " when his meditations are suddenly broken in upon. A little hand is laid confidingly on his arm, and a familiar voice says, pleadingly, " Footlights ! "

With a sudden start he turns round and cries, " Myra, what in thunder has brought you here ? "

" I've just come down on the train," remarks the little girl. " I've run away—there was a reward offered—I saw Teddy come to denounce me, and I fled from 'military discipline'! Take me to a place where they hire actresses—I want to be a child-star ! "

CHAPTER XI.

A T this startling proposition, Footlights gives a little yell of delight and says: "My! ain't you a dandy? But you'd better look out, or the Society for the Prevention of Children's Earning Their Own Livins'll get hold of you; they'd put you in an asylum."

"Why, what have I done?" whispers Myra, her eyes big with terror.

"Haven't time to tell you now!" whispers Footlights, leading her along in the pushing crowd. "I've got to find about that 'ere body!"

"What body?"

"Quit talking and come on! I think I recognize one of the officers of that society—he's right there—if he knowed what you were up to, going on the stage, he'd jug you, sure!" With these ominous words to his new-found charge, who is trembling at his warning, and excited and nervous at the strange scene—its great crowd of struggling baggage-agents, screaming hackmen, and hurrying people—he drags her out from the huge depot on to Forty-second Street, taking her along that thoroughfare in the direction of Broadway.

"'Tain't the most direct route to my quarter of the city," he says to the little girl, "but I want to git a squint at the news-boards of the up-town papers, and see if that 'ere body is found."

"Whose body?"

" Whiticar's ! He's stolen all your mother's money and committed suicide ! "

" Stolen all my mother's money ? "

"Yes—and yours also! Your mother'll soon be doing plain sewing or starving—one's just as bad as t'other ! "

" No, she won't ! " returns Myra, confidently. " Haven't I told you I'm going to be a child-star? Don't child-stars *always* support their mothers ? "

" Yes ! and the whole balance of the family too, I reckon ! " says Footlights, contemplatively. Then he suddenly whispers : " You'd better not say much about going on the stage *now !* You're poor, and that society'll get hold of you, sure. They sometimes let rich children go on the stage at up-town theatres, but when poor ones want to make bread and butter on the Bowery—no, siree ! Not for Joseph ! "

" Why, I should think the poorer they were, the more they'd need to work ! " answers Myra, astonished.

" So would 'most any one else ! " rejoins Footlights. " But it's necessary to have a pull—and the poorer you are, the less pull you have. Why, I'd bet Vanderbilt could put a ten-day-old child on the stage, and they wouldn't even ask him if he'd got a permit —but, now you're poor, you look out the society don't get hold of you. You'd go into an asylum, sure ; and the minute you were popped in by a perlice-judge, you'd be a goner ! "

" But my ma would get me out ! "

" No, she wouldn't ! The law says you'd stay as long as the society wanted to keep you ; no mother—no father—no court —nothin' could get you out but them newspapers. The society is scared to death of journals what print in big type, ' Another Outrage by the S. P. C. C.' And if the newspapers kept going for 'em for a month or two, you'd probably feel your mother's kiss again. Not that the society don't do lots of good, for it does ! I seen 'em take Jakey Rivets from his drunken dad ; and Sally Jinks from her stepmother, who would larrup her and make her steal beer for her at night; though it's mighty hard on poor children that has pluck and grit, and wants to work for 'emselves —but here's what I've come to gaze upon."

Thus cutting short his remarks on what Footlights and numerous other poor children in New York consider their natural enemy, that young philosopher drags his charge into the usual crowd that stands each evening in front of the up-town newspaper offices on Broadway, near Thirty-second Street, trying to get cheap news from the bulletin-boards.

Squirming about, without any great regard for the feelings or toes of other people, he wriggles himself into the front rank, and soon sees, in big script, the following:

ANOTHER GOOD MAN GONE WRONG !

Joseph Whiticar, the Lawyer and Peekskill Politician,

Suicides by Drowning at Coney Island.

HE HAD STOLEN ALL !

Still Trying to Recover the Body.

" Still trying to recover the body !" reads Footlights. Then he suddenly mutters, " *I'll help 'em !* " and drags Myra as rapidly out of the crowd as he had forced her into it.

She emerges from the crush with her dress disarranged, and her hat half off her pretty head ; but the boy is so eager, he doesn't notice her appearance.

" Have we got far to walk ?" asks the child, anxiously, trying to replace her hat.

" A couple of miles," answers young Higgins, carelessly, whose muscles, though small, are of whipcord.

" A couple of miles ? And I'm so tired !"

This last is a sigh of fatigue from the little girl, and, noting this, her self-appointed guardian says, suddenly : " We'll take the street-cars ; I can think better riding than walking, and I wants to think *hard !* " With this he carefully assists his charge into a Broadway down-town car, and, seating himself by her side, attacks two difficult problems that are troubling his youthful brain : one is to dispose of Myra in safety for the night till he can return the child to her mother, and the other is to find the voice that still lingers so familiarly in his ear—the voice of the man who had ruined his theatrical enterprise, and then punished him for smoking cigarettes—the voice of the lawyer in whose suicide he does not believe.

To do the second successfully, he must first dispose of his charge ; and he bends his mind to this affair at once with youthful energy. He racks his brain to think of some good woman to whose care he can trust Myra for the night while he can go out and search for the voice. This consideration takes time, for the boy's acquaintances among the fair sex in New York are very few, and these mostly of a desultory kind, produced by his connection with the theatre.

He has come to no conclusion in the matter, when he is aroused by the conductor's voice saying, sharply, " Fare !"

" For two !" answers Footlights, awaking with a start from his meditation ; and, rummaging in his pocket, he produces and presents to the street-car official the twenty-dollar bill Captain Heaton had given to him.

That functionary inspects the greenback with evident suspicion ;

finally, convinced of its genuineness, he says, offensively and inquisitively, "Where did you get this, boy?"

"What's that to you? It's good, and you take your fare out, and pass me the change—right quick!" answers Footlights, savagely, who does not like the insinuation in the man's voice.

"It's good enough," says the official, "*too* good for such a boy as you to carry; besides, I've not got money enough to change it."

"No? Is the company busted?" asks young Mr. Higgins, ironically, who, never before having been burdened with a twenty-dollar bill, has never discovered that change is not made in such amounts on street-cars.

"I'll—I'll pay! I've—I've got ten cents!" cries Myra, uneasily, producing a handful of coins.

"All right, I'll borrow it, sis!" says the boy, and hands the conductor the money. "Now, that twenty-dollar bill—I'll trouble you for it, sharp!"

"First, where did you get it?" says the man.

"Give me that bill or I'll have you arrested and taken right off this car. Quick! or I'll have you up before a perlice-judge, and tell him where *I* got it, and how *you* got it!" cries Footlights, whose experience of New York has made him anxious to finger his bill again.

Thus threatened, the man hands him back the money, and is leaving the car when Mr. Higgins calls to him, "Ring up those two fares quick on the indicator, or I'll report you—you can't knock down on the company this time!"

There is a little laugh among the few occupants of the car as the conductor savagely snaps the indicator bell twice, and slips out on the rear platform.

This encounter over, Mr. Higgins is about to go to thinking again, when Myra suddenly whispers to him: "Won't you get off here? I see a nice place where everybody's eating, and I haven't had anything since breakfast—I ran away before lunch, you know—isn't that a good place to eat?"

Following her gaze, the boy glances into Delmonico's *café*, at the corner of Twenty-sixth Street and Broadway.

"Yes, that's a prime place to eat, I am told," he chuckles; "but I don't regularly dine there—it's—it's a leetle above my pile, and I generally patronize one of our Bowery quick and ready's. I'll take you to Lyon's Restaurant, and we'll luxuriate. Meantime, I'm thinking of a hotel for you this evening; that's what's bothering me. Don't you worry about the meals—I'll fill you up in about twenty minutes—it's your hotel's on my brain!" With this Footlights relapses into meditation again, only waking up at Union Square to transfer himself and his charge to a Fourth Avenue car, and borrowing another ten-cent piece from Myra to pay their fare, as he doesn't wish a second discussion with another conductor on the subject of his twenty-dollar bill.

He is not interrupted by the little girl; she is absorbed in the unaccustomed sights of the Bowery at half-past seven in the evening, when that most bustling and picturesque, though not most aristocratic, thoroughfare of New York is just lighted up with its innumerable gas-jets and electric lamps, and the grotesque transparencies of its dime museums, with their Circassian beauties, double-headed apes, tattooed women, and other attractive curiosities, are beginning to dazzle the eyes and draw in the money of their patrons.

He stops the car opposite Lyon's gigantic restaurant, and as they step out into the glare of its electric lights the little girl astounds him, for she cries: "My, isn't this Fifth Avenue lovely? I've dreamed about it—now I see it's more beautiful than my dreams!"

11

"That's where I agree with you! This is the purtiest place in New York, though 'tain't gloomy Fifth Avenue, but the light, bright, and refreshing Bowery!" remarks Footlights, who is delighted to find himself once more in this cheaply brilliant but dearly beloved and familiar scene.

"There's Ikey Mordecai's, the boss tailor. He beats every Broadway and Fifth Avenue store in electric lights, four to one! He's a corker, he is. He can sell more clothes for five dollars than any man in New York. And there's Cobblestone & Brusher's, the dandy jewellers. They have diamonds that'll blind your eyes when they has an incandescent burner behind 'em!"

He would point out to her more of the surrounding points of interest, did not Myra say, suddenly, "Then this must be a very nice restaurant, isn't it?" and look longingly at the various tempting dishes displayed in its windows.

"It's the best on the Bowery!" cries Footlights, proudly. "Come in and I'll stand dinner." With this he leads the girl into the place, which is crowded with people, illuminated by electricity, and presents, with its hurrying waiters, a scene of brisk, active bustle, though the crowd is thinning a little, as it is now half-past seven.

The two seat themselves at a table, which, fortunately, has no other occupants, as the parties dining there have just finished and risen to go to their evening occupations.

After seeing his hungry companion's wants attended to—for Myra has ordered a straight-bone sirloin steak and mashed potatoes, being advised thereto by Footlights, who remarks that she'd better cling to chops and steaks, as it takes an *habitué* to hit the hashes on the right days—that young gentleman contents himself with a boiled "apple-dump" and hard sauce, a local luxury that he has not forgotten. This he soon finishes, and, obtaining the latest edi-

tion of one of the evening papers, digests the details of the Whiticar suicide, while the little girl is still occupied with her din-

MR. HIGGINS DOES THE HONORS OF THE BOWERY.

ner ; for Footlights is a generous host, and has persuaded her to indulge in a dessert of chocolate *éclairs* and ice-cream.

He soon discovers that the main points of the tragedy are briefly as follows :

It had happened between eleven and twelve o'clock in the forenoon at Somers's bathing-place at the upper end of Coney Island. The day had been warm, and, though late in September, quite a crowd had come down from New York to indulge in probably what would be their last bath of the season.

Among them was a man of genteel appearance, who hired a bathing-suit and went into the surf. His actions were not particularly noted by the attendants in charge, or the throng who were in the water with him, though he seemed to be an expert swimmer, for he swam out to the raft.

No particular attention was paid to him, as he seemed to be, though venturesome, thoroughly at home in the water, and to have plenty of confidence in himself; for he ventured a long way out into deep water. That was the last any one saw of him. His absence was not noted until nearly an hour after this, when every one had left the surf; then, to the astonishment of the people in charge of the bath-house, this man did not reappear.

A hasty search was made for him, without success. He certainly had not returned to the room he occupied in the bath-house, for his clothes were still there. In one of the pockets of his coat was found a *portemonnaic*, and among the papers therein a number of cards, bearing the name of " Joseph Whiticar, Peekskill, N. Y.;" a letter addressed to Mrs. Joseph Whiticar, of the same place ; also another communication, directed to Hockstatter & Burton, a well-known firm of brokers on Wall Street.

A protracted and thorough search not disclosing any traces of the missing man, Mr. Somers, the proprietor of the bathing-establishment, took in person the clothes, letters, also a gold watch and ring, left by the party, to Hockstatter & Burton. They unhesitatingly pronounced them to be the property of Mr. Whiticar, the Peekskill lawyer; and, on opening the letter addressed to them, were horrified to find that it contained the statement that he intended to commit suicide, being driven to that course by financial embarrassment. The letter addressed to his wife had been immediately forwarded to that lady.

Further investigation showed that he had made away with some large trust-funds in his possession.

Though search was still being made for the body, there was little hope of it being recovered, as the tide at the time Mr. Whiticar had disappeared was at the full ebb, and running rapidly for Sandy Hook and the ocean.

"All the same," meditates Footlights, "I don't think that Whiticar lost his life—that duck! He may have lost a suit of clothes, a gold watch and ring, but if he ain't lost that voice also, I've an idea that I'll find it good and strong in some of my haunts."

But how to visit his haunts, so long as he has Myra to take care of and protect?

As he glances at her, the difficulty of his problem comes more strongly home to him than ever, for he notes the beauty of the child, soon about to become a woman, and knows that the more lovely, bright, and fascinating his charge is, the more care she will need among the temptations, pitfalls, and dangers of this great city.

Unconscious of his anxiety, Myra looks up from the last of her ice-cream, and, balancing the spoon in her hand, says, brightly: "Where are you going to take me now? I'd like to see a theatre *so much!*"

"Would you? Then I'll take you to one." For an idea has suddenly come to the boy. He knows of an actress who has two

little girls, and he'll get her to take charge of Myra for the night.
And, saying this, he produces his twenty dollars to pay their bill,
though Myra proffers her handful of silver.

"No, it's my treat!" he says. "'Tain't often I git a gal rigged
out like you in first-class clothes. You looks as if you had come
from Paree, you does!"

This he mutters gallantly, and with a shamefaced glance of
admiration that makes the color come to her dimpled cheeks. For
the girl is robed in a light, pretty muslin, with a dash of color in
her sash and hat, and, with dainty boots and gloves, makes a picture
that causes Mr. Higgins to blush as he looks at himself ; the gar-
ments furnished him at the Bushnell villa being clean and comfortable but ludicrously incongruous, his costume being made up of a
pair of Arthur's knickerbockers, which are much too small for him,
and an old coat, vest, and hat of the defunct Mr. Bushnell, which
are equally too large.

A philosopher, however, doesn't trouble himself about costume
for any great length of time, and Footlights, calling a waiter, gives
him his greenback, telling Myra that he wants to break his bill, and
here he'll find no trouble to do it, as he is known.

This proves to be the case, as the waiter shortly returns with
the change.

While that functionary has gone on his errand, he suddenly
asks the girl : "Where did you get all your cash ?"

And her reply astounds him, for she simply says : "I took the
bank."

"What bank ?"

"My bank !"

"Your bank ? What are you givin' me ?"

"The truth ! My bank—my tin bank that I saved my money
in. I broke it open and took it all !" Thus being recalled to

thoughts of her home, Myra suddenly says: "Before we go to the theatre I'd like to write to mother and tell her I'm all right, and shall be a child-star, and take care of her now she's poor."

"I'll do better than that!" returns Footlights, who remembers the expression on Mrs. Bushnell's face when she reported the absence of her loved one.

"Better than that?"

"Yes, I'll wire your mother!" And, having received his change, he hurries Myra to a telegraph-office, from which he sends the following unique despatch:

NEW YORK. *Sept.* 30, 1887.

MRS. BUSHNELL,
        RIVER VIEW, PEEKSKILL.
I've caught her and she is all O. K. The body ain't found yet and I'm looking for it.
                                                            JAMES HIGGINS.

This being paid for, he leads her into the street once more, and pilots her carefully through its hurrying crowds, saying cheerily: "Now you will open your eyes, Myra, for I'm going to take you to a *real* theatre!"

"A *real* theatre! Wasn't your opera-house a real theatre?" asks the girl in surprise.

"Well, yes, for a country-town, perhaps it was," returns Footlights; "but, now I'm out of the show business, I don't mind acknowledging to you that it wasn't a marker on M. C. Martin's Bowery. We're in front of it now."

Looking round at his words, Myra finds herself gazing at a building blazing with electric lights. The front of the structure is embellished by lithographs that illustrate the woes of "Bertha, the Sewing-machine Girl," which drama, type bills and placards announce, is enjoying "A Phenomenal Run, and is a success! *Success!!* SUCCESS!!!"

Entering the glass portals of the building, Myra finds herself
in the lobby of the theatre ; this is not crowded at the moment, as,
the time being half-past eight, most of the audience are already
seated and witnessing the play.

Immediately opposite them stands the ticket-office, and, watching his chance when the treasurer is not engaged in waiting on late
arrivals, Footlights steps up to the open window, and whispers:
" Is my place filled, Mr. Chip ? "

The voice that greets him is rather stern—it says : " Jemmy,
we've been open two weeks ; why didn't you report at the beginning
of the season ? "

" Didn't know you was open—I wa'n't in town ! " Mr. Higgins's tone is rather humble for him—he's working to get back in
his old position, which means to him present bread and butter.

" Well, it's your business to know when our season begins.
You step back to the stage-manager, and if he hasn't got another
boy in your place, you can go to work to-night."

" O K," returns Footlights, and is about to take Mr. Chip at
his word when that gentleman suddenly asks him : " What were
you doing out of town ? "

The answer he gets astonishes him. " I was out on the road
managing a combine myself," replies Mr. Higgins, airily ; and,
seeing a smile on the treasurer's face, he takes advantage of his
opportunity, and asks for a pass for Myra.

" There isn't a seat in the house except in the boxes ! " mutters
the official.

" You usually favor managers with seats in the boxes—one of
them'll suit me." And Mr. Higgins begins an eloquent but short
appeal to his auditor, telling him Myra has been placed under his
charge by her mother, and he doesn't know what to do with her if
he goes to work right off.

Peering from his window, and affected by the bright face and pretty figure of the child as she stands amazed but interested at the brilliant scene about her—for even the box-office of a theatre is susceptible to beauty—Mr. Chip says: " There's a box-seat—you take good care of the little lady ! Step along now !" and, tearing off a coupon, he gives it to Footlights, for a little crowd has drifted in from the street, and is coming up to his window.

"Come on," whispers the boy to Myra. " You've seen how a manager works the free list ! "

"It must be a wonderful thing to be a theatrical manager !" mutters the girl, greatly impressed by Mr. Higgins's success at the box-office.

" It is," says that young gentleman, proudly ; but Myra hardly hears this last, for, passing the door-keeper, the wonders of the auditorium burst upon her view. Her tongue stops—she has only use for her eyes.

The great crowd, the brilliantly lighted stage, and the music of the orchestra all tend to daze this child, who has never been in a real theatre before. She hardly knows what she is doing, as Jemmy pilots her down the aisle, and, by the courtesy of one of its gentlemen occupants, gets a front seat for Myra in the box.

" You take in the performance," he whispers, "and don't leave here on no account till I come back. See you between the acts!" And before the girl realizes that she is alone, he is out of the box and in the main body of the house again. Here he hurriedly se- cures a programme, and, glancing over it, mutters : " Rosa's in the cast to-night. This *is* luck."

With this enigmatical ejaculation, he dives down a stairway that descends from the back of the parquette to a passage which, running between two rows of large dressing-rooms, immediately under the auditorium, leads him to the rear of the house, and so, by another stairway, to the stage itself. This passage is exclusively for the convenience of employees of the theatre on ordinary occasions ; though, in case of fire, it is intended for general safety.

Once upon the stage, Footlights reports direct to the stage-manager. That autocrat of "behind the scenes" is seated in his private office, and too busy to talk to him for any length of time. He shortly says : "Jemmy, you stay at that stage-door leading from the pool-room, and if any one asks for me, bring me his card. I expect a gentleman shortly on business."

To hear is to obey, and Mr. Footlights, once tyrant of The Peekskill Opera House, now humbly stands at one of the stage-entrances of a real theatre, doing what he is ordered.

There are two stage-doors to Martin's Bowery : one, the main entrance for scenery, company, and the general business of this bustling theatre ; the other, which is more properly a private one, for the use of the stage-manager and those who call to see him by appointment. The general entrance opens on the public street running in the rear of the building ; the private one, from the large pool and billiard room which is immediately back of the saloon that adjoins the theatre on its Bowery front.

It is at this latter door that Footlights is posted.

He has been in position for ten or fifteen minutes, and is already anathematizing under his breath the tardiness of the expected caller on the stage-manager, for Mr. Higgins is not of a patient disposition, and thinks he has a good deal of work to do this evening—when a faint and hesitating knock is heard upon the iron door.

" I know that kind of sound," mutters Footlights ; "that's the rap of some chap who'd like to git behind the scenes and has got no business to—some chap who would like to just say a word to some of our pretty actresses."

He consequently only partially opens the door, but as he does

so a very handsome bouquet and letter, as well as a dollar greenback, are slipped into his hand, and a low but earnest and im-
ploring tone comes to him, saying : " Please deliver this note and

these flowers to
Miss Rosa Living-
ston at once, and
say that I beg her
to see me, if only
for a moment."

As this voice
strikes his ears, he
shivers as if para-
lyzed, but clings
to the letter and
flowers, and con-
trives to gasp out,
"All right!" then
closes the door, and
sinks down on the
bare boards of the
stage, overcome.

After a moment
or two he recovers
himself sufficiently
to mutter, " Blessed
if Whiticar ain't our

" BLESSED IF WHITICAR AIN'T OUR DEAR OLD ' SOFTY ' ! "

dear old 'Softy' !" for the voice which had come to him with such
wonderful effect was the voice for which he was hunting—the voice
of the man who had thrashed him in the darkness—the voice of
his enemy—the voice of the body that was drowned at noon that
day at Coney Island.

CHAPTER XII.

RECOVERED from his partial syncope, Mr. Higgins reconnoitres to find if his voice has also revealed him to the gentleman he designates as " Softy," for at his gasp of " All right!" he thinks he remembers a faint start and tremble in the hand giving him the note and bouquet.

He cautiously reopens the door to a slight extent, and carefully squints out into the pool-room. The individual at whom he gazes has turned away and is watching a game that is in progress, though seeming to have little interest in either the players or their rolling ivory balls. He evidently thinks it is much too soon to expect an answer to his message, and is merely trying to kill time, though the uneasy, anxious manner in which he plays with his massive watch-chain plainly shows that he is nervous.

" Perhaps it's because he recognized me ; perhaps it's because he's so mashed on Rosa that makes him worried. My ! ain't he the biggest fool about her, and she an honest married woman with two kids, who won't even look at him. That's why we calls him ' Softy'!" meditates Footlights, as he inspects the man, who is dressed in an apparently ready-made but very new suit of clothes, and sports several diamond-studs on his bosom and rings on his fingers. Notwithstanding the night is warm, he wears a heavy overcoat, as if he intended travelling, and a high black hat which, drawn down over his eyes, indicates no wish to be easily recognized.

This gentleman, whose bouquet, letter, and voice have produced such an effect upon Mr. Higgins's nerves, had first made his appearance one night during the preceding spring, and had immediately become infatuated with Rosa Livingston's pretty face and charming acting. He had given himself out to be one George Lawrence Gardner, a wealthy stock-raiser from New Jersey, and as such laid siege to her heart.

As soon as she discovered his passion, Miss Livingston had refused all presents, and even communications, from him ; but thinking, as many men do, that an actress's heart is easy winning, her very disdain only seemed to add fuel to his flame ; so Mr. Gardner had persisted in his suit, and had displayed such humility and capacity to receive snubs, and even insults, from the object of his love that young Higgins and the other employees of the theatre had derisively nicknamed him "Softy."

Inspection can reveal no more to Footlights at present, for he has never in his life seen Mr. Whiticar to know him, and his only clew to this man's double identity is his voice, which is peculiarly nasal and penetrating.

"No danger of his running away—he's too dead mashed ! I'll deliver his message, and see if Rosa can give me a pointer as to 'Softy,'" mutters the boy. With this he takes his way to Miss Livingston's dressing-room, and, knocking on the door, is desired to enter by this young lady, who is a bright soubrette of twenty-four, a devoted wife and mother, and in private life is known as Mrs. Edward Pike Gibbons—Gibbons, her husband, being an actor of "leading juveniles" now on tour with a combination which is doing a repertoire of Mr. Daly's adaptations from the German.

She is in stage costume, and greets the boy with a kindly "Hello, Jemmy ! Haven't seen you before, this season !"

"No," answers Footlights, "and perhaps you wouldn't see me now if it warn't for 'Softy.'"

This name affects Miss Rosa Livingston very much as a red
rag does a mad bull ; she rises and, catching sight of the bouquet
and letter, cries : " Take those things out of my dressing-room at
once, and throw them in his face ! "

" Not till I tells you a story ! " returns Mr. Higgins, firmly.

" Take them away immediately ! "

" Not till——"

" I don't care if he has given you a dollar to deliver them,"
cries the actress, suspiciously.   " Out of my dressing-room ! "

" Not—till I tells you——"

" If you don't, I'll report you to the stage-manager.   *Move !* "
And, standing with one white arm uplifted, Miss Livingston makes
a very pretty, though somewhat stagy picture, for she is in ball
costume.

" Wait till I tells you a story ! " cries Footlights, not budging a
step.   " Listen to me, for the good of others ; you ain't hard-
hearted.   Rosa, listen to me for the sake of a little gal like your
own, who has been robbed ! Listen to me afore you fires his
letter out."

This appeal, made in a piteous voice, astonishes the actress,
who sinks into a chair, and says : " Go on, quick, for I'll be called
for the second act in ten minutes ! "

" Then," mutters Higgins, " I'll paralyze you in *five !* " and
astounds her, for he whispers, in melodramatic hiss : " HEARKEN
TO THE STORY OF ' SOFTY'S ' CRIME ! "

At this startling announcement the young lady gives a little
shriek and grows pale, while Footlights, in vivid, lucid, and ungram-
matical periods, tells her the story of his wonderful adventures in
Peekskill : how Myra is under his charge ; how Whiticar, who is
supposed to be dead in deep water, has " Softy's " curious voice ;
in fact, all that he suspects, guesses, or knows.

"HEARKEN TO THE STORY OF 'SOFTY'S' CRIME."

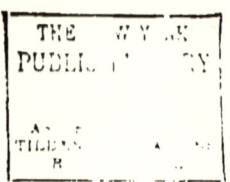

During this narrative, which takes perhaps five minutes, Rosa interrupts the boy but once, and that is with a suppressed laugh, as he describes the punishment he received for smoking cigarettes; but Footlights's face becomes so tragic at her mirth that she suppresses it entirely.

"Very well," she says, after a little pause of thought. "What do you want me to do?"

"First, I want you to take charge of Myra, and put her with your kids for the night. I wants to be sure that she's safe as if she was in a Deposit Company's vault, and I'd a coupon for her. You see, I must have my hands free to operate on 'Softy'!"

"Certainly, I'll take care of the little girl with pleasure!" returns the lady, thinking of her own little ones, and becoming motherly at the thought. "What else?"

"Then I wants you to open 'Softy's' letter."

"Certainly not!"

"Why not?" returns Footlights, savagely. "What harm will it do?"

"A great deal! Ever since that man made me the object of his persecution, I've refused his gifts, and have returned every letter from him unopened. You know that!"

"You bet!"

"If I open one now, he'll take it for encouragement and persecute me all the more!" At this thought the lady becomes angry, starts to her feet, and cries: "Oh, how I hate him! Why does he dare follow me?"

"It's because you're so purty," suggests Footlights, trying to pacify her with a compliment.

But Rosa has got to a point where compliments are of no avail. "No, it's not!" she cries. "It's because I'm an actress! I've got my reputation to guard for my husband's sake! If Mr. Gardner has

12

committed a crime the newspapers'll get hold of it, and the actress is always pictured as the siren, and the man—the poor, deluded, unsophisticated, innocent man of the world —as the victim. Bring me the little girl—I'll take care of her; but as for you and that bouquet and letter—out you go! OUT!"

"But, Rosa!"

"Not a word!"

"But, Ro——"

"Out, I say! *Quick!*" and with a vigorous shove the actress forces the arguing Footlights from her room, and, slamming the door in his face, locks it.

Hearing the click of the bolt, Mr. Higgins turns slowly away from the portal and goes to examining the letter he holds in his hand by the light of a gas-burner in an unoccupied dressing-room.

"It's got no postage-stamp on it!" he mutters. "'Tain't no crime against Uncle Sam;

"'SOFTY,' I'LL TAKE PITY ON YOU—I'LL MAKE YOU THE HAPPIEST VILLAIN IN NEW YORK!"

and then 'Softy' would feel *so* complimented. If he thought Rosa read it he'd feel real encouraged. I'll—I'll tickle his vanity," and with this young Mr. Higgins tears open the envelope and stares at the impassioned epistle of an old man who has been made half-crazy by love for a young woman.

It is several pages long and has been apparently very carefully composed. Some parts of it the boy hardly understands, though he thoroughly grasps these important statements among the frantic appeals and endearing expressions that surround them.

The writer, who is rich, knows that Miss Livingston is married

to a man who is poor. He thinks she smiled at him from the
stage the evening before, and therefore hopes that his persistent
love is not all in vain. Circumstances have placed him in a position that will permit him to make her his wife—that for business
reasons he is compelled to go to Canada; if she will either accompany him or will follow him there, she can easily procure, through
his money, a divorce from her husband and then he will marry
her. In case she chooses to accompany him she has only to
send to him for the railroad tickets, as he leaves by the eleven
o'clock train that night. Should she be willing to follow him she
has only to say one word, and any money she may want for the
journey is at her command. This curious document is signed,
"Yours till death, George Lawrence Gardner."

As the boy finishes his inspection, a grim smile comes over his
face, and he mutters : "'Softy,' I'll take pity on you—I'll make you
the happiest villain in New York !"

CHAPTER XIII.

THIS he proceeds to do with despatch. First, he throws Mr. Gardner's bouquet, which is a very striking affair, composed of a center of violets surrounded by white lilies of the valley, out of sight among a pile of disused and dusty armor in the property-room ; then he hurriedly seeks another boy employed, like him, about the theatre, for he fears recognition and suspicion if he delivers the message in person to Mr. Gardner. Finding this youth, whom he addresses as Smithy, he directs him to go to the stage-door leading into the pool-room, where he will see "Softy" waiting. He is then immediately to say to that gentleman, "Miss Livingston's comps.; and she'd like the tickets right off !"

"What do I get for this job?" remarks Smithy, who has an eye for business.

"What 'Softy' 'll give you, and you know he's generally liberal. But as ghosts walk, don't you take them tickets to Rosa or she'll murder us both ! You bring 'em to me."

Thus instructed, Smithy goes on his errand, and shortly returns in a most joyous but surprised state of mind.

"Did you deliver the message to 'Softy'?" asks Footlights, eagerly.

"Yes."

"What did he do ?"

"First he kinder reeled and fainted and scared me ; but soon I sec'd it was with joy. He was 'most like a maniac with happiness.

He pulled out of his pocket-book these railroad tickets, gave 'em to me, and said : 'To Miss Rosa, with my dearest love. Ask her to remember, eleven o'clock sharp.' Then he pulled out a busting big roll of greenbacks, and gave me a bill."

" How much was it ? "

" Five dollars. You said I could have the whole of it !" mutters Smithy, putting his hand in his pocket as if to be sure of the money.

Here Footlights astounds him, for he says : "So you can. Give me the railroad tickets, and I'll fix the matter with Rosa."

This wonderfully liberal offer " Smithy " snaps up eagerly, and, departing, leaves Footlights examining his tickets.

They are a series of coupons entitling the bearer to a passage from New York to Montreal, Canada, *via* the New York, New Haven & Hartford Railroad to Springfield, Massachusetts ; the Connecticut River Railroad to Newport, Vermont ; the Passumpsic *route* to Lenoxville, Canada ; and the Grand Trunk from there to Montreal.

This inspection pleases the boy greatly. He mutters : " Now I've got ' Softy's' route and destiny, and, by George ! the railroad tickets to follow him with, if I wants. All the same, it'll be better he don't leave New York. Now I'll show him to Myra ; if she recognizes ' Softy ' as Whiticar, that'll settle his case, sure. I reckon the police would arrest him on her swearing to him."

With this the boy passes through the long alley running between the dressing-rooms under the auditorium. Then, ascending the stairs at the back of the orchestra, he finds himself once more among the audience.

All these operations of Footlights have taken some little time ; the curtain has just fallen on another act of the woes of " Bertha, the Sewing-machine Girl," and a good many of the spectators are filing out for a breath of fresh air, or refreshment of some other kind.

Elbowing his way past these, young Mr. Higgins is soon at the box in which Myra is seated, and the little girl, apparently in the highest spirits with the delights of the drama, turns a beaming face to him, and says : " I've never had so nice a time in my life ; you're awfully kind to bring me here. This performance is even better than those at your Peekskill Opera House ! "

" Glad you weren't lonely," mutters Footlights, with a grin.

Then he whispers in the girl's pretty little ear : " Now, Myra, I'll introduce you to the lady who'll take care of you to-night," and leads the girl from the box to the front of the house, determined in some way to give her a sight of the so-called Gardner, of Martin's Theatre, and see if she recognizes him as Whiticar, of Peekskill, before he places her under the sheltering wings of Mrs. Edward Pike Gibbons.

Footlights, as soon as his charge is in the lobby, cautiously tells Myra of his wonderful discovery with regard to " Softy's " voice, and leads her to a spot where he expects she will get a view of that individual ; but to his disappointment Mr. Gardner is not to be seen. He makes a hurried but thorough search of the theatre, dragging Myra about with him in a reckless and desperate sort of way, but fails to find the individual for whom he is looking.

After a few hurried inquiries from the employees of the building, Footlights concludes, from what he learns, that Mr. Gardner, after receiving the joy-inspiring news from Smithy that his pursuit of the pretty actress was to be crowned with success, had apparently left the theatre in a state of supreme bliss to make his arrangements for his trip to Canada.

" I'll catch him at the depot," he mutters to Myra. "Come,

little girl, I'll put you in charge of Mrs. Gibbons, and then I'll be free to tackle 'Softy.' "

"Can't I go with you to the depot to see if he *is* Mr. Whiticar?" says Myra.

"Yes, of course! That's my ticket!" he answers, suddenly; but a second after mutters : "No, you must stay right here with Miss Livingston ; I might have to leave you and light out after him to Canada!" For, the instant he turns the affair over in his mind, he is convinced that he dare not at this time of night risk taking Myra to the Grand Central Depot unless accompanied by Rosa ; and that the very explanation of how he acquired his knowledge of Gardner's intended movements would fill that lady with unmeasured rage. " I reckon she'd take my head off if she knew that I'd opened her letter and accepted for her Gardner's railroad tickets to Montreal. No!" he mutters, "the last round'll have to be between 'Softy' and me—with the perlice as umpires and referees."

With this he leads Myra behind the scenes to Miss Livingston's dressing-room, and, without further discussion, leaves her under the care of that lady, charging the little girl to do what Miss Livingston tells her, and informing her that he'll telegraph her mother, "and she'll be down in the morning to look after her and put her on the stage in prime shape." The last he utters with a choked-down chuckle and a wink at the fair soubrette.

"You know, Miss Livingston," babbles Myra, "that I'm going on the stage to be a child-star as a matter of duty."

" Duty!" gasps the actress, astonished.

"Of course! Now mother's poor, I must take care of her. All child-stars support their families, I'm told."

"Yes," returns the soubrette, " their mothers make them ; but your mamma, I hope, has too much pride to live off your precocity, my dear."

Then she says to Footlights: "Don't wire Mrs. Bushnell my address at the theatre—let her come to my home; you can remember it by this," and she gives him her card.

Miss Rosa Livingston,

Soubrettes
and
Leading Juveniles.   214 *Henry Street.*

On reading this, Mr. Higgins's face assumes an expression of deep meditation; then he walks hurriedly out, and, going into the unused dressing-room, thinks so hard it gives him a headache. His mental struggle lasts, perhaps, for ten minutes; then he utters a yell of triumph like a Comanche Indian, and chuckles, "'Softy,' you can say your prayers, for you're jugged!" Next he pops Miss Livingston's card in his pocket, and, running to the property-room, searches anxiously among the old armor where he has thrown Mr. Gardner's floral offering. This he finds nearly as fresh and beautiful as when it left that gentleman's hands.

Armed with these, he is about to bolt from the theatre, when he suddenly pauses and mutters: "He'd never suspect Smithy; he'd believe every lie he told him." Having uttered these enigmatical words he hunts up Mr. Smithy again, with a vague idea that this young gentleman may be perhaps useful to him in carrying out a plot that is, as yet, only half-conceived in his brain, but the very audacity of which promises success.

Coming on the boy, who is watching the play from the wings, he leads him to one side and whispers, " Can you get off to-night?"

" As easy as you kin, now the play's a-running !" rejoins young Smithy.

" Then you come with me—I've got fun ahead for you !"

" What'll I get for it?"

" Whatever ' Softy' gives ! Reckon it'll be more than a fiver !"

" My goodness ! more than a fiver?"

"Yes, you'll make him so tarnation happy this time. Come on !"

Then, leading the way from the theatre, Footlights, accompanied by Smithy, boards an elevated train for the Forty-second Street Depot. On their way up, he has great trouble in satisfying his companion's curiosity as to their movements ; in fact, at one time Mr. Smithy becomes so frightened at some hint of Footlights that he manifests a desire to bolt the whole business, and is only kept in the traces by the remark that "Softy" 'll surely go more than a fiver this racket.

Arrived at the Grand Central Depot, Footlights looks at the clock ; it is half-past ten.

Finding he has ample time for all his arrangements, he first puts Smithy out on the street, with directions to report the moment he sees Mr. Gardner coming : then goes into the telegraph-office and sends a message to Mrs. Bushnell, calculated to allay all anxiety in regard to Myra, though he cautiously says nothing about Whiticar, judging that it will be safer not to mention that gentleman's name about the station to any one until he has him where he wants him ; *i.e.*, behind the bars of some police-jail, in New York.

He knows that, upon his unsupported statement as to the similarity of Gardner's voice with that of the supposed suicide and

embezzler, no police-captain would dare to take the responsibility
of making the arrest. The risk of a mistake would be too great.
"They'll be more apt to jug me," he meditates, as he looks at his
clothes.

His only hope is to have "Softy" arrested for some other
offence that will keep him under lock and key till next morning.
By that time he can get evidence that will surely identify him.

Suddenly an idea passes through his brain. What if Gardner
isn't Whiticar? He gives a shiver of fear at this, and for a moment
half resolves he won't take the risk ; but, even as he does so, the
recollection of the sympathetic eyes and kindly words of the woman
who had that day protected him from a brutal attack, and soothed
his sorrows with tender hands and ministered to his wants with
benevolent hospitality, comes to this friendless boy, and he deter-
mines that, risk or no risk, danger or no danger, by no chance shall
the rogue who has defrauded and robbed her and her little children
escape, if he is alive, with his plunder.

"Don't think it would do me much financial harm, if 'Softy'
did get fifty thousand dollars damages agin me for false imprison-
ment," he chuckles, as he nerves himself for his part in the comedy
he proposes playing.

The portion of the Grand Central Depot in which this must
necessarily be enacted is the waiting-room from which passengers
take the trains running over the New York, New Haven & Hartford Railroad, the tracks of which company carry nearly all the
traffic between New York and New England ; besides various local
trains that run to suburban towns along the line.

The last of these accommodations—until the trains for the benefit of parties returning from the theatres of the great city to their
homes in Mount Vernon, New Rochelle, Larchmont, Greenwich,
Stamford, etc.—is about leaving. Its passengers fill the waiting-

room with a noisy, bustling crowd ; but very shortly most of these present their tickets to the officials at the doors leading to the track, and soon the room is comparatively empty.

The next train that will leave is the eleven o'clock, the one Mr. Gardner had mentioned in his letter. This is the through Boston express, only stopping at Bridgeport, New Haven, Meriden, Hartford, Springfield, and one or two large towns in Massachusetts. Any one arriving in the waiting-room can now reasonably be calculated upon intending to go out on the Boston express. This is perfectly well known to Footlights, who has studied the time-table, and has not been bashful about asking questions of the railroad officials. He now begins to look around for somebody who will assist him in placing "Softy" behind the bars of a New York police-station.

Casting his eyes about with this view, a sudden look of astonished joy comes into them. On a bench near the exit to the train stands a medium-sized hand-satchel ; upon its yellow leather side in plain black, easily-to-be-distinguished characters are painted two letters, " R. L."—the initials of Rosa Livingston.

"This *is* a streak of luck!" he mutters, then turns his eyes to the presumable owner of the baggage. She is a tall, grim female. who wears spectacles and carries another small satchel and umbrella. "She'd have never let go of that large one if she didn't have her hands full. She is a strong-minded female, a woman that would go through fire and water to put a man-tyrant into a tight place. She'll do ' Softy ' up, if I can only play my game proper!" he thinks.

Contemplating this picture, Mr. Footlights's face becomes one subdued chuckle of joy and triumph ; he has been racking his brains for some certain plan to hold "Softy" in New York till Captain Heaton can get a sight of him, and see if he is Whitcar.

To accomplish this he has, in the last hour, turned over in his mind every situation in melodrama, comedy, or tragedy that he can remember ever having seen, read, or heard; and this grip-sack marked " R. L.," and this angular woman with the umbrella, have just shot into his mind a scene from a little farce, " *To Paris and Back for Five Pounds,*" that he thinks will do the business.

He goes quietly to the telegraph-office, and there writes upon Miss Rosa Livingston's card these extraordinary words : " Please take my bouquet and satchel to the train." This he ties to the flowers sent to the actress by Mr. Gardner, and returns to the waiting-room.

Glancing at the clock, its hands indicate seven minutes to eleven ; at the same moment his heart gives a big jump, for Smithy comes quickly to him and reports " Softy " as entering the depot.

A second after, Mr. Gardner runs panting in, and hurriedly takes his place in line at the ticket-office, apparently intending to get his ticket first, and find his lady afterward, as his time is now short.

He is, fortunately, so much engrossed in forcing his way to the window, which is now besieged by a little crowd, that he does not notice Footlights or Smithy. Shrewdly calculating that it will take Gardner all of three minutes to buy his ticket and get out of the crush, Mr. Higgins proceeds rapidly and effectively to do his work. He walks to the bench upon which the satchel initialled " R. L." stands ; this occupies the middle of the settee. The woman to whom he supposes it belongs is seated at one end ; Footlights carelessly takes possession of the other.

He studies the woman ; she is restlessly awaiting some one, and growing impatient and anxious, as the time for the train's departure grows near. Nonchalantly placing the bouquet upon the satchel, taking care that the card attached is in plain sight, he saunters out

of the door on to Forty-second Street. There beckoning Smithy to
him, he gives his co-worker the following lucid instructions : " The
moment I tips you the signal, post yourself by that 'ere bouquet,
and catch ' Softy's ' eye—he'll be looking 'round and will spot you as
soon as you do him. Then you point to the flowers, and say, ' Miss
Livingston wants you to bring her bouquet and baggage to the
train—she couldn't carry it all, and that ticket-taker wouldn't let
me pass the door.' That'll make ' Softy ' more happy than an
elected alderman, and he'll perhaps stand a tenner ! Quick ! Remember, when I takes my hat off and wipes my brow."

With this, Footlights walks rapidly back to the owner of the
satchel, and says : " Marm, there's a person outside with a
sprained ankle who is asking for a lady with a grip-sack marked
' R. L.'"

" Yes, my brother !" cries the woman. "Take me to him instantly. We may lose the train !" And, springing up, she runs
across the waiting-room to the Forty-second Street sidewalk.

Footlights follows her, but as he reaches the door he turns his
head and sees Mr. Gardner, who has just purchased his ticket,
gaze eagerly about the station. Then *he makes the signal.*

Smithy bolts to "Softy's" side, and whispers to him a few
words. The man steps to the bouquet, and recognizes it as the
one he had given Miss Livingston ; the next instant he is reading
her card. With a look of ineffable joy he picks up bouquet and
hand-satchel, and is marching toward the door leading to the train,
the proudest and happiest scoundrel in New York.

" ' Softy's ' hooked, if I'm judge of a woman's face," chuckles
young Higgins, with a hideous grin. The next instant he hears a
man's gruff voice saying : " My ankle sprained ! Who fooled you
with that trick ?" Then to his ears come the yells of spinsterhood
aroused, and a cry : " Stop that scoundrel in the brown overcoat,

just getting his ticket punched ! He's stealing my satchel ! Stop him. He's got a confederate ! Seize him ! QUICK !"

This last is well uttered, for Mr. Gardner at this moment makes a desperate but fruitless attempt to pass the ticket-man and run for the train.

The next instant escape is hopeless ; he is collared by half a dozen by-standers and station-hands, including a young new and ambitious Irish policeman.

Mr. Gardner, brought to bay, gives a little shiver, and begins explanations, each one of which adds to his apparent guilt.

" I assure you, my good woman," he says to the lady of the grip-sack, " this satchel belongs to a young lady under my charge—Miss Rosa Livingston. Observe, this bouquet is hers; I presented it to her myself to-night; this card is hers also. Now look at the initials, ' R. L.,' hers also—Rosa Livingston."

" Rosa Livingston ? You sneak-thief !" cries the woman. " Rachel Lawton ! That's what they stand for—my name ! See, I've the key to it ! I can give a description of what's in it before opening it." This she hurriedly does, and, unlocking the satchel, her statement of its contents is found to be correct.

"That settles yez !" cries the Irish policeman. " Ye're wanted, my man !" and would drag the hapless Gardner away without further ado, but the prisoner cries out, desperately : "It's all some horrible mistake—Miss Livingston is on the train and can explain it !"

" See if she is, and be quick about it, for it's near leaving time !" commands the policeman.

A search is hurriedly made by the porters of the cars—and word is brought back, "No Miss Livingston on board !"

Then, as the gates are about to be closed for the departing train, Gardner grows very pale, and cries again : " Keep me from leaving

MAKING "SOFTY" HAPPY AT THE GRAND CENTRAL DEPOT.

now, and it's my business ruin! How much bail do you want?"
wildly offering a roll of greenbacks.

"Money won't get ye off!" cries the policeman, very savagely.
"Don't try to bribe me in-public!" and he sternly also compels
the woman and her brother to remain and make a complaint
against the prisoner.

But here something occurs that clinches the matter, and settles
all apparent doubt of Gardner's guilt. Footlights, growing too
interested, oblivious of personal safety, forces himself into the front
rank of the crowd.

He is hardly there when the woman, catching sight of him,
gives a cry of triumph, and shrieks: "Seize that boy! He's his
accomplice!" and, before he realizes it, young Mr. Higgins is also
in the clutches of the law. The accusing spinster hurriedly states
how he lied to her to lure her away from her property while the
older villain stole it. Two by-standers corroborate her tale.

"What are yez doing about here, anyways, boy?" asks the
policeman, suspiciously.

"This railroad ticket'll show!" gasps Footlights, producing the
one delivered by Gardner for Miss Livingston's use.

"Why, he was going exactly the same route as his pal," cries
the ticket-puncher, who still holds in his hand the one proffered by
Gardner at the gate.

"The same route and the same distination—that settles it. No
more words!" says the policeman, and, assisted by another officer,
they drag Footlights and Mr. Gardner to the sub-station, followed
by the complaining witness and a detachment of the crowd, among
whom is the amazed and terrified Smithy.

This young gentleman lingers about the depot and police-
station, in a dazed kind of way, until he hears some one remark:
"There's another boy in that gang they arrested to-night, I'm told."

13

This has such a fearful effect on his nerves that he disappears, and isn't even seen at the Bowery theatre for ten days.   At the end of that time, however, he sneaks into that place of amusement in a half-starved condition, where he receives a very warm welcome from his father, who is the janitor of the establishment.

CHAPTER XIV.

ARRIVED at the sub-police station of the Twenty-third District, which is immediately under the railroad depot, and is entered from Vanderbilt Avenue at Forty-fourth Street, the charge is entered against the two prisoners; they are brought before the sergeant in command, the captain being temporarily absent, and are hurriedly searched. This operation discloses upon the person of Footlights the remains of the greenback Captain Heaton had given him, some eighteen dollars and fifteen cents, as well as the usual boy's belongings, and a pack of cigarettes and matches to ignite the same; and reveals upon the body of the man who gives his name as George Lawrence Gardner a roll of bills, amounting to some eight hundred dollars, and little else save a pocket-knife, lead-pencil, and a bunch of keys.

This disclosure horrifies Footlights; he had expected to see produced from the pockets of his suspect, certificates of deposit, bills of large amounts, bonds, and other securities; in fact, a goodly portion of the property Whiticar had embezzled from the estate of Mrs. Bushnell. This is a fearful disappointment to the boy, who now meditates with concern, and even repentance: "Is poor old 'Softy' my innocent victim?"

The gentleman's anxiety to be admitted to bail, however, soon awakens his suspicions again. Mr. Gardner says, quietly: "I presume five hundred dollars will be sufficient security for my appearance to-morrow morning, sergeant? Please take that much of my roll, and give me the balance to liquidate my hotel-bill to-night."

"You'll have to wait till the captain comes in before you can be bailed," says the police-sergeant, politely.

"I'll furnish a thousand dollars," utters Mr. Gardner, eagerly.

"I can't talk to you about bail till I see the captain."

"Two thousand in *cash !* "

"There's only eight hundred in your pile," says the police-official, looking rather curiously at the prisoner. "I hardly see how you'll get it. I don't know of any midnight banks in this precinct. If I did, they'd be faro-banks, and I'd close them very quick."

After this sally, the sergeant, who is a humorist, gives a little chuckle, and looks at Mr. Gardner, who breaks out, excitedly and anxiously : "I can get it. *Three* thousand ! I can't—I won't sleep in a cell all night !"

Now this anxiety of the prisoner makes the police-sergeant suspicious. He says, shortly : "I would not take the responsibility if you offered me ten thousand—you must talk to the captain. Here he is !"

At this the autocrat of the precinct, a fine-looking man of, perhaps, forty-five, enters. Mr. Gardner turns to him and eagerly explains the matter.

"You must take bail ! The crime of which I am accused is, of course, petty larceny. No one would value the articles in that satchel I am accused of stealing at over twenty-five dollars !" he cries.

This disparagement of the spinster's wardrobe does not add to that lady's good temper. She cries back, angrily : "*You* may value them at what you please, but *I'll* swear they are worth a hundred."

"That settles it! Grand larceny!" says the captain. "No bail after nightfall for felony."

"But, captain——"

"I can't discuss it with you!" returns the police-officer, firmly but courteously. "That's the rule! You'll have to wait for a judge to bail you to-morrow morning." Then he turns to Footlights, who has been an interested though silent witness of this conversation, and asks: "What have you to say about the matter, boy?"

Here Mr. Higgins gives the police-captain a shock; he returns: "I decline to make any statement without the advice of my lawyer."

At this one or two policemen, listlessly looking on, snicker, as the captain gives a little meditative whistle, and says: "You're a young hand and cool hand. So cool a hand, I reckon you've been behind the bars before. There's only one unoccupied cell. Lock 'em both up in it."

As this order is about to be executed, Mr. Gardner suddenly says: "As I've got to spend the night in a cell, I presume you don't mind my putting on my overcoat again, as it's rather cold."

No objection being made to this, the gentleman resumes his outer garment, of which he had been deprived during the search. Then the two are led to the cell, and locked in together for the night, Footlights making himself comfortable in a corner, but Mr. Gardner pacing uneasily about, and sometimes smiting his hands together as if in despair, and now and then uttering sighs that almost end in groans.

So the night moves on, young Higgins's mind upon but one problem: "Is this man the supposed suicide, Whiticar, or is he not?" Once or twice he has hopes he has made no mistake, for, Gardner's eyes being turned upon him, he fancies he sees a flash of recognition and rage in them, but this is so rapidly forced into an expression of almost cynical indifference that he nearly doubts he saw it.

Desperately anxious to set his mind at rest, for he knows he has little time for action if "Softy" is really Whiticar, Footlights rummages in his brain for some expedient to settle the question. Chancing, also, from very force of habit, to place his hand in his pocket, in search of one of his nicotine mental stimulants, he finds a portion of a broken cigarette in the corner of that receptacle, also half a match—fortunately, with the head on it. The commonplace nature of these articles, together with their being only remnants, at that, have caused them to be overlooked in the search.

As Footlights's fingers run over these, a sudden test of Gardner's identity flies into his mind : " Old Philosophy himself couldn't stand such a tackle," he thinks, and in an instant his practised hands have fished out the cigarette-stump from his pocket, and lighted it.

Mr. Gardner has by this time tired of his promenade, and is seated in a kind of despairing trance. Footlights walks straight up to him and puffs the smoke full and square in his face, three times.

" What did you do that for ?" cries the man, rousing himself.

" What did I do that for ?" repeats young Mr. Higgins. " I puffed that 'ere cigarette-smoke in yer face, 'cause yer can't lick me for it here as yer did the other night in yer son's bedroom in Peekskill."

But in this he is mistaken. The words have hardly left his mouth when, with a yell of rage, the man is upon him. " You miserable spy !" is hissed in his ear, and he is picked up and dashed against the side of the cell again and again. He struggles desperately, but not silently, for he knows murder will scarcely appease this man's rage, and so screams with all his lungs for help. This soon comes to him ; the door is thrown open, and two or three

SMOKING "SOFTY" OUT.

stalwart policemen enter and tear the man-brute from the boy-
victim.

" Take me out of this cell, or he'll murder me," pants Footlights, with torn clothes and bruised limbs, but with contented joy
in his eyes.

" What have you done to him to make him act like a maniac?"
asks one of the officers.

" I only smoked a cigarette in his face," laughs young Mr. Higgins ; but at this remark such a fearful look comes into "Softy's"
face that the policemen pull the boy into the passage and relock
the door on Mr. Gardner, who is pacing up and down the cell like
a caged tiger.

This disturbance being reported to the captain, he has Footlights
brought to him, and says :   " What's the matter between your pal
and you? There's something I don't understand. You'd better
make a clean breast of it."

" I will, to-morrow, after I've seen my lawyer," answers the boy,
and he asks leave to telegraph Captain Heaton at Peekskill. As
ample money had been found on his person to pay for the message, permission is granted, and Footlights sends the following
despatch :

SUB-STATION, 23D PRECINCT, N. Y.,
Sept. 30*th*, 1887.

CAPTAIN HEATON,
    RIVER VIEW, PEEKSKILL.

Come at once to me at present address. If you can't get down by nine in the morning,
telegraph your lawyer to come and see me—for I've got what you want.

JAS. HIGGINS.

This being sent, and Footlights being accommodated with a
chair in the waiting-room at the back of the station, he lies down
thereon, muttering : " 'Softy' was Whiticar ! That 'ere cigarette
smoked him out of his hole !"   Then he goes contentedly to sleep,

for he knows some one will shortly come who can recognize the lawyer by his face.

This happens sooner than he expects. At six o'clock in the morning a police-officer shakes him by the shoulder, and tells him a lady and two gentlemen want to see him in the office. These prove to be Mrs. Bushnell, Cyril Heaton, and his lawyer—a gentleman of reputation and prominence in the legal profession.

Footlights's first telegram had been delivered to Mrs. Bushnell at 10 P.M., after the last passenger-train had left that day for New York. This she had, of course, shown to Captain Heaton, he having remained at Peekskill to aid in the search that was being made in the town and surrounding country for the missing Myra.

The information received by the first telegram had greatly relieved the mother's fears; and the second telegram, coming at eleven, had calmed her so much that Cyril had succeeded in getting a good deal of information from her about the property that was in Whiticar's hands, when, a little after twelve o'clock, Mr. Higgins's last telegram came. Being addressed from a police-station, new fears for Myra sprang up in Effie's heart, and she implored her *fiancé* to get her to New York, in some way, at once. Though not alarmed as to the little girl, Cyril was very anxious to know what Footlights had to disclose. Consequently, finding that a freight-train would leave at 1.30 A.M., he, by the kindness of its conductor, embarked Mrs. Bushnell and himself in its caboose and wired his lawyer to meet him at Footlights's new abode.

So all three are now in the police-station, awaiting his explanation.

"My child! Where is she?" cries the mother, getting hold of Footlights in a pathetic way, and fondling him as she implores him.

She does this in such a melancholy way that she alarms the boy, and he in turn frightens her, for he cries: "Great Scott! What's happened to Myra? Why are you blubbering over me? Isn't she at Henry Street, as I telegraphed you?"

"I haven't been there! When I found you were at a police-station, I—I didn't know——"

"Oh!" answers young Higgins, quite relieved. "Then Myra's all O K; I guarantees Miss Rosa Livingston *nee* Mrs. Edward Pike Gibbons. You'll find your girl a-dreaming of you, I reckon."

At this Mrs. Bushnell gives the boy a sudden kiss, and cries: "God bless you for taking care of my poor child!"

"Perhaps she won't be so *awful* poor, after all. I've been taking care of some one else," mutters Footlights. "Just get the perlice to show you what I've got in that 'ere cell. Go and take a look at him arisen from the dead!"

"You mean Mr. Whiticar!" gasps Mrs. Bushnell.

But while she has been speaking, Cyril and the lawyer have had a few hasty words with the police-captain, and all three have gone to see the arrested man.

From this visit they come back more or less excited, for Heaton has immediately recognized the supposed suicide. In fact, Whiticar has not denied his identity. He has simply said: "If it wasn't for that infernal boy, I'd have been out of danger by this time."

Turning to Footlights, the captain of police says, rather sternly: "Why didn't you tell me whom you suspected the prisoner to be when you saw me considering the matter of letting him bail himself out? I'd have had him identified in an hour. Don't you fail to trust the police next time. We're not so bad as the newspapers make us!"

"Yes, why didn't you tell him, Footlights, and he could have sent for Myra? She would have recognized Mr. Whiticar immediately," remarks Mrs. Bushnell.

Here Mr. Higgins astonishes them all, and greatly confuses Effie. He gets red and then pale, and, finally, turning his face away, stammers out that he wouldn't like to think of Myra ever having been one minute in a police station-house.

At this the police-captain gives a low whistle, and says: "By the head inspector, if the young bantam ain't a sentimentalist!" then walks laughingly away.

Before any other remark can be made on this subject, however, the lawyer drives out sentiment by suggesting: "We must take immediate action to replevin the property, bonds, etc., Whiticar had on his person at the time of his arrest."

"I rather think he must have shipped most of his stealings by some other route to Canada," returns the police-captain. "He had only eight hundred dollars on his person."

" No bonds ? "

"No other valuables whatever except his watch, chain, and some jewellery."

At this the lawyer's brow clouds a little, and Heaton looks very serious.

A moment after the police-captain says: "He must have command of more funds. He offered to put up three thousand dollars in cash as bail last night. Where could he hope to get the money from ? "

Then Footlights cries—a wild idea striking him: "Out of his overcoat! When he was trying to squeeze me to death, and I a-fighting him, it crackled like crisp paper was in it, whenever I grabbed it ! *Replevin his overcoat right off!*"

Under this suggestion, Mr. Whiticar's overcoat is immediately investigated, with astounding results. It is lined with greenbacks of large denominations, government and railroad bonds, as well as other convertible securities; in fact, in it is found the great bulk of Mrs. Bushnell's fortune. These are all, of course, taken charge of by the police-officials, while Heaton's lawyer goes out to take action to attach and replevin the same, as well as to enter charges of fraud, embezzlement, and forgery against the prisoner. And before the city courts are opened there are complaints enough against Whiticar, as the Irish police-justice remarks, to " hould the Quane of Shayba!"

This judicial gentleman, after hearing Mr. Higgins's very curious statement as to his actions of the night before, sums up his case as follows :

" It's very ivident, young man, you've committed a crime. I can't tell exactly what crime it is, but as ye meant well, and it's yer first offence, I'll not be too hard on ye. If ye grow up as smart as you've begun, you'll be fit to be a newspaper detective some day. Tin dollars or tin days !"

The "tin" dollars are immediately paid by Captain Heaton, and Footlights becomes a gentleman of leisure once more.

As for Whiticar, investigation proved that he had swum direct from the bath-house, where he had left his wearing-apparel and jewellery, to another one, where he had deposited a second suit of clothes. Hastily dressing, he had taken the train, and was in New York City when his absence from the first bathing-establishment was discovered ; thus, by the loss of a few valuables, producing a belief in his suicide. His case was sent to the Grand Jury, which soon after indicted him ; but before his trial and conviction nearly all Mrs. Bushnell's property was recovered from him, it being much easier to make a rogue disgorge when he is behind prison-bars than when he is safe across the Canadian line.

Though Mr. Footlights was a free man, he did not return at once to the Bowery theatre, being rather dubious as to how his use of her card and name would be received by Miss Rosa Livingston. But in his evidence he had given her such a good character, and had so described the soubrette's haughty rebuffs of "Softy's" importunities, that the newspapers fortunately held that charming actress up as a marvel of domestic worth and noble motherhood, to such a degree that it materially aided her in her profession ; and, noting this, Mrs. Edward Pike Gibbons showed she was a woman of sense by, after a time, forgiving young Mr. Higgins.

CHAPTER XV.

SOME six weeks after Footlights's night of adventure in New York City, on a bright November morning, the church-bells of Peekskill ring out their wedding-chimes. On the afternoon of this day young Mr. Higgins, in a suit of clothes the like of which had never graced his form before, stands on the veranda among the crowd of guests at Mrs. Bushnell's or, rather, Mrs. Heaton's villa, for the charming Effie has this day given her hand to the gallant captain of the Twenty-second.

Surrounded by beauty, wealth, and fashion, the representative of the cruder civilization of the Bowery has felt himself not altogether at home. True, he has been treated like a hero—and his return to Peekskill has been that of a conqueror. In the light of his New York success his local failures have been forgiven him ; for, as long as the American people are what they are, the man or boy who saves and defends womanhood or childhood from the attacks of avarice and crime will always receive their praises, their blessings, and their hands in fellowship. So this day would be a happy one to Footlights, if he felt at his ease and among his equals. But in this educated and refined company, though not of a bashful temperament, and attempting his finest stage manners and etiquette, Mr. Higgins feels, to use his own expression, " outclassed."

Three of the uninvited watch the pageant from the convenient fence of the Rawson villa. They are Teddy, Bob Savage and little Tommy Try. As they look on their former leader " putting on airs," as they term it, his glory fills their childish souls with undisguised envy.

THREE OF THE UNINVITED.

"I'm sure they had ice-cream at the wedding-breakfast," whispers Tommy Try, very sadly.

"Did they?" says Teddy, with a little groan. Then he mutters,

"GIVE ME EDUCATION, CAP! THEN, PERHAPS, I WON'T BE TOO SMALL FOR MY BOOTS WHEN I
COME BACK AND——"

savagely: "First thing he knows, that Footlights 'll find himself too small for his boots."

The object of their remarks is oblivious to their censure: he has drawn away from the throng, and is sadly meditating upon his past greatness when he had been a theatrical manager in the old barn he called the Peekskill Opera House, the roof of which he can just see among the tree-tops—or when he held the great title of Head-center, and proudly boasted he carried the destinies and happiness of the town in his grip-sack.

From this revery he is awakened; Cyril Heaton, coming quickly to him, wrings his hand, and says: "I've just time to make you a proposition, Jemmy, before I leave with my bride on our wedding-tour. I want to thank you that to-day her children are not paupers, and for the care you took of Myra when she made her little flight to New York."

"Don't say nothin' about that, Cap.," says Footlights, returning the gentleman's squeeze.

"But I must," continues Cyril, "for I am deputed by my wife to act in this matter for her. She has commissioned me to put aside a sum of money to be invested for your benefit. Now, I'll either put this money into property or education for you. Which do you choose?"

"You kinder take my breath away, Cap," says the boy, as, forgetful that he has a handkerchief in his pocket, he brushes a tear out of his eye with the sleeve of his coat; "I know a variety show that's as sure to make money as Barnum." For wild dreams of being a future Tony Pastor have suddenly struck his brain.

As he says this, Myra comes on to the veranda. Elaborately dressed as she is, in white, in honor of her mother's wedding, she looks more of a woman than she has seemed before. The autumn sun is in her brown hair, the joy of love and trust in her hazel eyes;

for she has learnt by this time that she has no better friend on earth than the man who has this day taken her mother's happiness into his hands.

She cries: "Jemmy, have you been lost? I'm afraid you've been lonely among all this crowd of grown-up people, to-day. I've been looking for you. Mother wants to bid you good-by, and thank you for being kind to me—when I was going to be a child-star."

As she comes toward him, the boy's vision seems to span the future and see another wedding-scene on this very spot, and another bride and groom. He cries: "Captain Heaton, give me education. Use that 'ere money sending me to school!"

"Yes, and to college, too!" returns Cyril, heartily.

"Then," mutters the boy to himself, "perhaps, with education, I'll be like one of them, and won't be reckoned too small for my boots, if I come back and ask—" Here he looks at the little maiden and blushes, and his heart gives a great thump of joy, for Myra's sweet face seems to be illuminated with an answering rose-tint.

Is it merely girlish modesty, or some forecast of the passion of coming womanhood?

FINIS.

www.ingramcontent.com/pod-product-compliance
Lightning Source LLC
Chambersburg PA
CBHW020612030726
47497CB00007B/2203